KT-420-829

13

GUNS OF THE SIOUX

GUNS OF THE SIOUX

Tom Curry

CHIVERS
THORNDIKE

This Large Print book is published by BBC Audiobooks Ltd, Bath, England and by Thorndike Press®, Waterville, Maine, USA.

Published in 2006 in the U.K. by arrangement with Golden West Literary Agency

Published in 2006 in the U.S. by arrangement with Golden West Literary Agency

U.K. Hardcover ISBN 1–4056–3796–X (Chivers Large Print)
ISBN 13: 978 1 405 63796 6
U.K. Softcover   ISBN 1–4056–3797–8 (Camden Large Print)
ISBN 13: 978 1 405 63797 8
U.S. Softcover   ISBN 0–7862–8724–1 (British Favorites)

The text of this Large Print edition is unabridged.
Other aspects of the book may vary from the original edition.

Set in 16 pt. New Times Roman.

Printed in Great Britain on acid-free paper.

British Library Cataloguing in Publication Data available

Library of Congress Cataloging-in-Publication Data

Curry, Tom, 1900–
        Guns of the Sioux / by Tom Curry.
            p.   cm.
        "Thorndike Press large print British favorites."
        ISBN 0–7862–8724–1 (pbk. : alk. paper)
        1. Dakota Indians—Fiction. I. Title
    PS3505.U9725G86 2006
    813'.52—dc22   2006010234

CHAPTER I

Forbidden Land

Near the rugged summits of the great Black Hills, two bearded prospectors stared at one another in wild surmise.

'Gold, Jem!' rasped the taller man hoarsely. 'Gold to the grass roots!'

'Yuh're right, Al. We're rich as kings!'

They were in a narrow, tortuous gulch, concealed from any spies who might be in the distance, and had entered the Hills secretly, eluding the soldier guards of the United States Army. For this was forbidden ground to whites, sacred to the mighty Sioux nation. But the lure of gold had drawn them irresistibly.

For the moment they were wildly elated, with visions of what the future would mean, once they took the precious metal to civilization. They had no hint that fierce eyes were watching them from the brush-fringed rim of the ravine; could not guess that but a few short minutes of life remained.

The country was a veritable paradise, the Black Hills of southern Dakota. Bold and rugged peaks thrust their summits to an azure sky. The mountain flanks were clothed in dark Scotch pine, which had caused the first explorers to so name these mysterious slopes.

Deeded to the great Sioux nation in '68, settlers were not supposed to encroach on the reservation. Here, at special seasons, the red men came to hunt, to cut lodge poles and to propitiate the Great Spirit they believed dwelt in the heart of the Hills. Those terrible, sudden thunderstorms, the reverberations of mighty sounds, and the flamboyant flash of chain lightning playing about the somber peaks could mean nothing else to the savage heart. The inner deep canyons were shunned by the Sioux.

Valleys were carpeted by wild flowers of every hue. Pines, cedars, aspens, box elders, burr oak, grew in profusion, as well as wild fruits, cherries and plums. Bear, panther, mountain sheep, wolf, deer, beaver and buffalo teemed in the vast preserves.

To the west the Great Plains extended all the way to the Rockies. Southeast were the Bad Lands, strange-colored buttes in pastel shades, furrowed and mighty, tinged coal-black, scoria-red, deep-green, with a grayer fringe of cactus, and flesh hue, all like some unevenly woven Indian rug. Columns of clay supported masses of sandstone which had protected them from erosion. Gothic spires, and chalk cliffs, windows, minarets, beehives, all manner of bizarre rocks were in the Bad Lands. Then the country stretched flat to the Appalachians, with the Black Hills the only break between the continent's two chief ranges.

'No wonder the Indians want the whites to keep outa the Hills,' chortled Jem, turning the big nugget he had found over and over in his calloused palm.

'Yeah, they savvy there's gold in here.'

Neither man ever spoke again. Jem suddenly threw up his hands, the chunk of yellow metal flying into the air. A bluish hole appeared between his eyes and he died on the spot, folding up at his partner's boots.

The rifle crack was still echoing through the deadwood gulch as Al, gaping at the falling corpse of his friend, was whipped around by the impact of the long slug that hit in under his left shoulder-blade, biting his heart. His head snapped back, teeth clicking as he collapsed on Jem.

For a time there was but the wilderness silence, the soft kiss of wind on dry brush. Then the crackle of twigs and sliding gravel warned of someone approaching.

Three men rode down the steep clay slope into the gulch. The leader was large, and the first thing that caught the eye was the Indian head-dress of feathers he wore. His pants were fringed buckskin, and his hide was burned, dark-stained. His cheeks were smeared by yellow and red stripes, his mouth painted thrice its normal size.

The rider directly following him was a lean Indian with the round, high-boned face and hawk-beak of the Sioux. He wore deerskin, and carried a hunting knife in a doeskin belt. He also carried a modern pistol in a cartridge belt, and in one bony red hand gripped a Winchester carbine, while he guided his wild paint horse with knees, a rope noose loose in his free hand.

A single eagle feather was in the band about his straight ebon hair. His eyes glowed black, fierce, and scars on his breast told that he had undergone the Sun Dance, torture ordeal of the Sioux.

He shoved ahead, slipped lithely from his blanket pad and bent over the two prospectors.

'They done for, Spotted Fawn?' growled the man in the head-dress.

'Ugh, Great Chief, all dead,' replied Spotted Fawn.

The man in the feathered head-dress swung in his saddle, grinning back at a burly hombre who brought up the rear. That man had a wiry black beard, a ragged black mustache, and matted long hair. His face was wide, the nose squashed flat against a thick upper lip. Small, red-rimmed, shifty eyes gleamed from the hirsute growth. The torso of 'Kansas Joe' Murphy, as men knew him, was immense, but his legs were short and bowed.

He was clad in a buckskin jacket and dark pants which were tucked into high, muddy boots. But he had crumpled up his wide

4

Stetson and stuck it in his saddlebags, and now wore a narrow band and an Indian feather.

At close range it was plain two of these riders were disguised as redmen. At a distance, if they chanced to be spied by patrolling soldiers or scouts, they might easily pass as Sioux hunters.

'Well, Murphy,' remarked the 'Great Chief,' as Spotted Fawn had designated him, 'yuh been claimin' Charlie Reynolds is the best shot in this country. What do yuh think of my aim?'

'That was a beaut,' agreed Kansas Joe, shifting his tobacco cud from one cheek to the other. 'And Spotted Fawn ain't no slouch with a carbine, either!'

The Chief dismounted, stooped to pick up the big. gold nugget dropped by the dead Jem, turned it over and over, gloating on it.

'There's gold all around, boys! This is the best spot yet! C'mon, we'll smooth out all signs here, then drop this vulture bait near the trail.'

'I can't see how yuh expect to work it,' grunted Kansas Joe, shaking his shaggy head. 'The Black Hills was given to the Sioux forever, and the Army throws out settlers and prospectors. How yuh figger on snakin' 'round that?'

'I'll get 'round it,' promised the Chief. 'With enough "incidents" such as this one, and with the country excited over the gold strike that we'll let leak out, the government'll be forced to abrogate that treaty. We'll be on the inside, and take what we want, savvy? This gulch is worth a million by itself. It'll be ours.'

'Huh!' growled Kansas Joe Murphy. 'Ain't a bad idee. It'll take time and cash, though, Chief.'

'Yeah, but it'll mean we'll own Dakota. I haven't much more time to spare this trip, Murphy, so we'll have to organize fast. Collect yore pards, and Spotted Fawn'll rouse the Sioux at the right moment. Wait'll Red Cloud and Sitting Bull hear whites're pourin' onto their sacred ground!'

'Ugh!' agreed Spotted Fawn. 'Sitting Bull heap love fight!'

'Murphy,' the Chief went on. 'You get busy right off. Set up a camp on Cherry Crik, west of the last settlement. We don't want to be too close to other towns. A store, warehouse, a saloon, tents, and shacks'll do. We'll have men on the Missouri to steer settlers there, urge 'em into the Hills, and sell 'em the supplies they need, cheap, right on the spot.'

'But, Chief, where'll we get enough supplies to start with?'

'I've got a little cash, and yore boys ain't finicky about who owns what, I hope. I'll tell yuh how to find the supplies, all we want. C'mon, let's get outer here. Spotted Fawn, scalp them two and we'll drop 'em on our way,

6

so they'll be found by the army patrol.'

Grandiose plans that dazzled Kansas Joe Murphy evolved from the disguised white man's evil, clever brain. Plotting wholesale murder and thievery, the Great Chief rode eastward out of the Hills, trailed by his henchmen.

There would be many more dead. This was only the start. Blood was to stain the virgin soil of the Black Hills, blood of red men and white . . .

Several weeks later, at Fort Abraham Lincoln, outpost on the upper reaches of the Missouri in Dakota, two U. S. cavalry officers hurriedly crossed the bare, wind-swept parade ground.

The Seventh Cavalry was stationed at the fort, and infantry was along the frontier. The post was located in a valley, and just back of it was a long chain of bluffs. The river was in front, and the settlement of Bismarck across the Missouri.

Quarters for six companies stood on the side of the parade ground nearest the stream, and detached houses for officers opposite. There was a long grain-storage structure and a guard-house. Quartermaster and commissary storehouses for supplies, and the adjutant's office completed the square. Some distance on were the log huts of the Indian scouts and their women and children, and a level plain for drill.

The post had been built before the railroad was finished and the houses had been made of unseasoned wood, with ceilings and partitions of thick paper. The lumber usually warped and in the bitter winters of Dakota it was difficult to keep warm.

Blue-clad soldiers, Indians in handsomely beaded buckskin and feathers, civilian scouts, and soldiers' wives, could be seen at the big military post. Stables for six hundred cavalry horses and various other structures necessary to the life of the garrison had been set up.

The two officers quickly went to a square-cut house and were ushered into a room furnished with as much coziness as the rough life permitted. There were buffalo and bear robes on the crude floor, and animal heads on the walls.

A man sat at a desk in the center of the room, and the two who had entered stiffened to salute.

General George Armstrong Custer, the man at the desk, was about thirty-five, tall and lithe. He had tawny hair and a bushy, drooping mustache of the same hue. He was a handsome, dashing figure of a man, and it was known that wherever Custer was, there also was flamboyant life. In his private life he was as fun-loving as a youth, but as a commander he was a stickler for discipline and military etiquette. Many adored him, many hated him, but no one denied he was a great soldier and leader.

He was angry now, his deep-set eyes burning.

'I have gone over your inventory, Captain Winters,' he snapped. 'Comparing it with my theoretical lists from Washington, I find that tons of military supplies, both from the commissariat and the quartermaster divisions, are missing.'

Captain Frank Winters, to whom he spoke, was a burly man, older than the general. For, at the age when most young fellows are starting out in life, Custer had been a major-general in Sheridan's cavalry during the Civil War.

Winters had sandy hair and his face was inclined to softness. Now his brown eyes widened, but military discipline did not permit him to do more than reply to his superior's questions. He dared not show his feelings. His close-clipped mustache twitched, however, as Custer smartly dressed him down.

Wilted by Custer's lashing tongue, Winters gulped, 'Yes, sir,' saluted, about-faced and left. The general turned to the other officer.

'Sit down, Major Clyde,' he said more mildly. 'I have important news. There have been a number of Indian massacres reported from the Black Hills. Prospectors are entering the Sioux reservation there, despite our efforts to prevent it.'

'It's a serious situation, sir,' Major Clyde

9

agreed.

Major Hanson Clyde, attached to Custer's staff, and entrusted with important missions by the commander, was a tall, precise man. A year or two older than Custer, his massive head was crowned by fine black hair, curling at the ends. His broad nose, dark eyes, and wide mouth over a strong chin, gave him an austere appearance. In neat blue uniform, sword belt and shining cavalry boots, he was every inch the soldier.

It was Custer's habit to make his plans in secret, and then move with efficient speed. Such plans he now had ready.

'We are to make an expedition into the Black Hills, Major,' he said briskly. 'The War Department has had many complaints against the Sioux. Settlers have been killed, and there are strong rumors that gold has been discovered in the Hills. I have drawn up instructions for each officer which I expect to be carried out to the letter.'

'Yes, sir.' Clyde's voice was deep, pleasant.

He accepted the written orders passed him by his commander, saluted, and took leave of General Custer.

For a time the great officer sat deep in thought. Then he rang a bell and an orderly came in, snapped to attention.

'Orderly,' commanded the general, 'ask Mr. Reynolds to report to me at once.'

CHAPTER II

A Plea to Pioneers

Billy North, scout and hunting guide in the western wilderness, rode his black gelding up the rutted, single street of a tiny settlement west of the Missouri River in central Dakota. A crude sign proclaimed its name: Cherryville. This little 'town' on the north bank of Cherry Creek was the edge of white civilization. Toward the sunset lay the strange Bad Lands and beyond, the forbidden Black Hills.

Curiously North's grave brown eyes took in the handful of rough-built shacks with sod roofs, and the old army tents facing across the road.

A crude sign over a semi-open structure said:

Kansas Joe's Whiskey and Beer

Another place proclaimed:

Hunting and Prospecting
Supplies—Provisions

Behind this latter was a windowless, barn-like warehouse, with a padlocked door.

The stalwart form of Billy North, latest

11

arrival in Cherryville, was encased in buckskin hunter's clothing. He sported a coonskin cap on his light hair, the tail proudly flapping over his left ear. In a belt he carried cartridges for his revolver, and under his left leg rode a Sharps .50 caliber buffalo gun. He was clean-shaven, his cheeks bronzed and smooth, in his first twenties, pleasant-faced, eager, and strong, Billy North felt that the whole world was his oyster, to be opened as he chose.

'Funny layout, all right,' he murmured.

Five miles east lay an older camp, so that there seemed little reason for this one, but they were doing a good business. And from a price sign set outside the store where another sign proclaimed that 'Soupy Lou' Griggs was the proprietor, goods were much cheaper than at other towns in the territory.

Merchandise had to be freighted up the Missouri, and then carted overland to the wilds of Dakota, so prices were necessarily high.

North noted a number of big covered wagons and teams that stood in the open spaces around the store—a pioneer train headed west—as he naturally gravitated to the store himself. He wanted to buy some canned delicacies, for he had been out guiding a hunting party for the past month, and craved the tidbits 'civilization' could offer. Canned peaches, for instance.

Dismounting, he flung his reins over the hitchrack and went into the store, built of raw timber. Inside was a jumble of barrels and boxes, tools and all sorts of supplies.

The store was crowded with people buying food and implements. Billy North lounged near the front door, watching. As he looked, a slim young girl, trim and vivacious, came out from behind a tall pile of goods and turned toward him.

North's eyes snapped open wider.

Her curly black hair was banded by a blue ribbon, and she wore a blue gingham dress with a white belt, and small slippers. A sunbonnet hung from one hand, though she was pleasantly tanned. She was beautiful, North thought, and felt an electric thrill as she appraised him with merry, dark, eyes.

'I need a new bonnet, Jake,' she said to one of the men making purchases, and her voice was soft and musical.

Billy North decided that the 'Jake' to whom she spoke must be her father. He was a man in his forties, bluff and heavy of body, with hair gray-tinged at the temples, a wide mouth and strong nose, and a chin beard clipped short.

'Yuh're always wantin' a new hat or dress, Edie,' he drawled to the girl, smiling, 'but yuh can have it, dear. Pick what yuh wish.'

She smiled at him, her even white teeth dazzling. She wasn't over seventeen or eighteen, thought North.

13

Along came a ratty little man, slight of body, with a receding chin, an uneven brown mustache, close-set eyes and sparse sandy hair. He wore a dirty canvas apron and black boots.

'Anything else, Mr. Burton?' he asked the man with the girl, eagerly. 'Yuh don't wanta be caught in them Hills without full supplies.'

A clerk, waiting on another man called :

'Hey, Soupy, how much for this new flour?'

'Twenty-five dollars for fifty pounds,' replied the ratty man.

'He must be the store owner, Soupy Lou Griggs,' mused North. 'And talkin' about "the Hills"! Wonder if them folks would be fools enough to head into the Sioux reservation?'

The thought perturbed him, especially so because of the pretty white girl. The idea of her falling into savage hands was not nice.

He edged closer to the man he had heard called Jake Burton. The chatter of voices rose in the store. The people who had just arrived in Cherryville were merry as children at a fair, as they bought what they needed at Soupy Lou's.

There were about forty of the pioneers, the majority of them stalwart, clear-eyed, bronzed fellows, and a sprinkling of women, who would follow their men through hell and high water, to victory or death, no matter what threatened. The raw, dangerous land was no place for weaklings.

14

A few older children, from twelve to fourteen, silently, watched the proceedings. There were no small ones. No doubt young offsprings had been left with relatives, while the parents went ahead to settle and build homes. These people were all in the same party, all clad in buckskin or homespun, sturdy Americans seeking fortune on the dangerous Frontier, buoyed by hope and brave hearts.

'Howdy, Mister,' North said to Burton in a low voice. 'My name's Billy North. I'm a hunter, and I know these parts and the West right well.'

Jake Burton turned grave eyes upon him. North felt that he was flushing, not so much from Burton's scrutiny as from the fact that his speaking to Jake had caused the pretty girl to notice him.

Burton stuck out a toil-calloused, big hand, and shook with North.

'Glad to meet yuh,' he said. 'My name's Jake Burton. I'm boss of the wagon train yuh see out there. These are my friends . . . Oh, Sloan!'

A young man in buckskin and moccasins stepped silently up. He had curly blond hair, fair skin, clean blue eyes. He toted a Sharps buffalo rifle, .50-caliber.

'This is Jed Sloan,' Burton told Billy North. 'He's a hunter like you, North. Kept us supplied with game all the way from Yankton on the Missouri.'

North and Sloan shook hands. Billy North felt oddly jealous, for no rhyme or reason, except that Sloan was mighty good looking. And Billy North envied him his position in the wagon train with Edith Burton. He felt better when Sloan introduced a young woman.

'This is my wife Georgia, Mister,' Sloan said.

Folk on the Frontier had a habit of open-handed interest and help toward each other. Burton's people clustered around North, and shook hands with him, asking questions about the country of Dakota. Billy North could tell them a lot.

He took them all in an honest, good-hearted lot, with no cravens among them. There were two dark, lean brothers, Ben and Ike Ulman, with mustaches and sideburns, and wearing blue pants, shirts, riding boots, and flat hats. Ike had his young wife with him.

Among the older men, 'Uncle Dan Olliphant stood out. He was Burton's chief lieutenant, a stout man with a round, bearded face, cheeks as red as apples, and always laughing. His wife 'Aunt Nenny,' was motherly and large and talkative.

They were North's kind of folk, daring Americans ever surging from the crowding East to the challenge of the West.

When they had shaken hands with Billy North, and ex-changed remarks, they went back to buying from Soupy Lou Griggs' clerks.

North could not say that any of Griggs' assistants compared in looks with the pioneers. They were pretty tough, despite canvas aprons which hid their guns.

' 'Tain't none of my business, Burton,' Billy North said to Jake, 'but I heard yuh mention the "Hills." Yuh ain't figgerin' on goin' in the Black Hills, are yuh? They're mighty dangerous. The Sioux don't want whites there, and if the U. S. Army patrol catches yuh, they'll burn yore wagons and chase yuh out.'

Burton's eyes narrowed as he stared full at North. For a moment he resented Billy's unasked-for advice, but seeing that it came from an earnest desire to help, he relaxed and then grinned.

Soupy Lou Griggs had waited, smoking a black cigar, while North met the pioneers of Burton's train. And as North warned Burton against the Black Hills, Griggs' dirty face went beet-red. His close-set eyes blinked with sudden rage.

'Well, dawggone my worthless hide, if yuh ain't got yore nerve with yuh, young feller, advisin' yore betters!' Griggs cried harshly. 'In this country we like men that mind their own business. Quit annoyin' grownups that savvy the world betten'n a wet-behind-the-ears hoss thief!'

North's under jaw went out. He scowled at Soupy Lou who blinked and stepped back a bit, quickly looking around for

17

reinforcements.

'These folks are headin' for Nevada,' Soupy Lou added. 'Ain't that so, Burton?'

'We're shore pointin' that direction,' said Burton. 'Thanks for yore warnin', North. I appreciate it.' He winked at Billy North as he added, in a low voice: 'We don't scare easy, yuh know.'

'I savvy that,' North answered, 'But—don't go into the Black Hills!'

Soupy Lou scratched his sparse-haired head and a couple of tall men, with guns strapped on came sauntering over and flanked Billy North.

Edith nudged Jake Burton.

'Oh, yeah,' Burton said. 'Meet my niece Edith. Name's Burton, like mine. Let's have a drink later, North. Jest now I better get my buyin' done.'

Billy North looked into Edith Burton's smiling eyes. She was the loveliest creature he had ever seen. And, knowing what went on under the surface around the forbidden Hills of the Sioux, he was fearful for her, convinced that the Burton party intended to enter the Black Hills, secretly, to prospect for gold. He was aware that the whites felt that they were blocked by the red men, while the Sioux felt that the whites were ruthlessly crushing them. It was an unfortunate time, with the barbarian and nomadic Indians being forced to give way to ever-encroaching and better-armed

18

white men.

'Will yuh please let me offer yuh some good advice, Ma'am?' begged Billy North humbly. 'I know all this country, have hunted through it, and I savvy the Sioux. They won't have whites in them Hills. It's sacred ground.'

'You seem mighty worried about us and the Indians,' said the girl. 'We've been able to take care of ourselves. Jake's had a good deal of experience with savages.'

'Yeah, but the Sioux are a mighty nation. Dangerous and tough. They got thousands of warriors. Stay outa the Black Hills!'

Aware of the glares of Soupy Lou and the nearby roughs, still Billy North sought to dissuade the Burtons from venturing into the forbidden territory. He spoke earnestly, depicting the perils to be found in the Hills.

Suddenly one of the armed men lurched against him, knocking him sideward so that he came down hard on the toes of the other hombre.

'Ow!' howled the other gunman. 'Watch where yuh're steppin'!'

He shoved North off, and the first man snarled:

'What's the idee, bumpin' me?'

'Look out, he's goin' for his gun, Burns!' yelled the second.

Billy North had intended nothing of the kind but decided he'd better, although it was too late. Burns' Colt barrel was already clear

19

of its leather holster, rising to pin the tall young hunter in buckskin.

Edith Burton's eyes widened in alarm, and a sharp cry rose in her throat. Her uncle, Jake Burton, had his back to the fracas, absorbed with his friends in other matters. Soupy Lou's eyes twinkled with triumphant amusement as he saw the two he had called up baiting the man who dared horn in on his affairs.

This instant-fraction was one for death, the sudden end that comes when armed men clash in combat. Those who lived by the gun usually died by the gun, and the man who prided himself on his quickness and shooting ability must soon prove it. For the Frontier resorted to such means to settle even slight disputes such as the color of a man's hat or the way he drank his whiskey.

Martial law existed around army posts of the wilderness. General Sheridan was in command of the district, while General George A. Custer, Brevet rank, Colonel of the 7th Cavalry, newly created after the Civil War, was stationed at Fort Abraham Lincoln. But in such a camp as Cherryville, there was no law or sheriff to protect the populace. Men looked out for themselves.

Billy North knew all this and sought to beat Burns, the blackbearded gunny, to the shot. He seemed in a fair way to make it, but a shove from the other gunman finished him for good.

A revolver shot roared in the store.

CHAPTER III

Riders of the Frontier

To Billy North's astonishment, he felt no stinging bullet to bring death. Instead, 'Blacky' Burns' slug kicked up splinters in the rough-laid boards between the stalwart young hunter's spread boots.

'Hell and damnation!'

That was Burns, shrieking with pain. The browned-steel pistol clattered at his feet, and he danced around, gripping his shattered right forearm with his left hand. His mate, stunned by the turn of the affair, looked back over his shoulder, hand dropping to his gun butt.

'Hold it, feller,' a cool voice ordered. 'Hold it, ' 'less yuh want to dance with yore pard.'

A man stood in the open front door of the store, an Army pistol in his right hand, from the muzzle of which drizzled blue smoke. It was he who had sent the quick one which had saved Billy North's hide.

All eyes turned on this new master of the situation. He was not a big fellow, although his shoulders were broad, and tapered to the narrow waist of the fighting man. Just about the ideal weight for a cavalryman, Captain

21

Robert Pryor, known better from Kansas to the Mexican border and the Rio Grande as the 'Rio Kid,' stood with spread feet, his black army boots with their short spurs firmly set. He wore a Stetson, the brim not so flowing as the usual cowboy's, cocked at a rakish angle on his close-cropped, chestnut-haired head. Under it blue eyes, filled with a devil-may-care, reckless light, gazed on the gathering in Soupy Lou's. His nose was straight and his chin firm, smooth shaven.

A three-inch, black leather belt was snapped tight at his waist. One holster was empty, the gun in his hand. He carried two others in shoulder holsters.

Unlike so many Frontier characters, the Rio Kid was as neat as a pin. Whenever he had the chance he looked as though he had just been turned out from a bandbox. He had acquired that from his army training during the Civil War when he had ridden as a scout for Custer. A genius at scouting, at gunfighting, hardened to peril and with death a familiar companion, the Rio Kid knew how to take care of himself under any circumstances.

There was about him an air of command, of the officer. A look at him impressed. Those wiry, whipcord muscles had the speed and agility of a panther, and showed it.

As the howls of the wounded Burns quieted, and the smoke drifted rapidly to the low ceiling of the store, several others of Soupy Lou's contingent started forward.

'Says who?' a gunny growled.

'Says this!' the Rio Kid laughed, his hammer spur back under his thumb, for he shot with a lashed trigger, the weight of the gun cocking the weapon as it came up, the hammer falling when he raised his thumb.

'Says thees two also,' remarked a boyish Mexican's voice from the window.

Outside stood Celestino Mireles, the Kid's trail comrade and follower, who owed his life to Pryor and who had sworn to go with him to the end. The Rio Kid, whom he always called 'General,' was his idol.

Bony and slim of body, Celestino had a rare spirit, brave and faithful. Black, straight hair showed under his fancy sombrero, and he wore bell-shaped, fancy pants, a short velvet jacket, and a red sash in which were stuck pistols and the long knife he loved. His large black eyes that could burn with a fanatic zeal were set deep in his thin face.

The 'two' of which Mireles spoke were the double barrels of the sawed-off shotgun with which he covered the flank of the enemy faced by the Rio Kid.

Outside, the late afternoon sunshine was yellow over the wild Dakota land. Shadows were cast long over the single street of Cherryville, and night was not far off. Close to the front door, behind Mireles, stood the dun

23

with the black stripe down his back, 'the breed that never dies.' Saber, the fast-stepping cherished mount of the Rio Kid.

Saber took a bite out of the hide of a mustang tethered near. He loved to fight, was army-trained, and had carried the Kid through dangerous forays in the war as well as afterward on the Frontier. The dun was not handsome. He looked rather angular with his long legs, yet the Kid had never come up against another mustang that could catch up with Saber when he really wanted to run.

Save with his master, Saber had a cayenne-pepper disposition. Now his big teeth were bared, and his eyes gleamed wickcdly. One was rolling in anger as the other horse sought to elude his bites and kicking hoofs.

'Nobody'll get hurt,' the Rio Kid declared slowly, looking over the men in the store, 'if he keeps meek-like and don't, reach for any firearms. How are yuh, Billy? Ain't seen yuh since the fracas at Adobe Walls.'

'Howdy, Rio Kid,' cried North, delighted.

'Step out of the door,' ordered Pryor. 'Anybody who wants to come, all right.'

But only Billy North accepted the invitation. Jake Burton's party was safe enough there. They were customers of Soupy Lou's.

'So long, Ma'am,' Billy North called to Edith Burton. 'I'll see yuh again, I hope.'

She was watching with large eyes, her face

sober but relieved. He thought she was glad he had escaped injury.

The frozen gathering in the store relaxed, as the Rio Kid, North and Mireles, guns ready, backed off. They grabbed their horses and mounted, riding down the road.

'What was the rumpus about, Billy?' the Kid inquired.

'Oh, hell!' replied North, with a shrug. 'I figger that party of pilgrims mean to sneak into the Black Hills, Kid. I was warnin' 'em off, when that sidewinder picked a fuss and drawed on me. That's all.'

'I savvy.' The Kid looked back over his shoulder. 'Steady, Saber,' he ordered, as the dun sought to nip at North's black.

Mireles rode the Kid's other flank, his sharp, dark eyes darting from side to side.

'Mucho bad hombres, General,' he muttered. 'Fun-nee town, *si.*'

'Yuh're right, Celestino,' agreed North. 'It's a queer camp. Run by a feller named Kansas Joe Murphy, whose rep ain't so clean in these parts. Fact is, I understand he used to ride the owlhoot trail. That Soupy Lou Griggs is a pard of his, I reckon. They got a bunch of helpers, too. Must be coinin' money.'

'Huh!' grunted the Kid.

He swung the dun, who shouldered North's black over to the long hitchrail in front of Kansas Joe's saloon, where a couple of dozen saddle horses stood, reins over the rack.

25

'What yuh mean to do?' asked Billy.

'I'm mighty dry, Billy. We rode a long way. Figger a drink would hit the right spot.'

'All right.' North shrugged. 'I'm with yuh. But if there's a rumpus, don't say I didn't warn yuh.'

The sun, ruby and low over the Black Hills, ducked suddenly from sight. Gloom was settling over the wilderness. The low purling of Cherry Creek, bounding Cherryville, hummed an undertone to the raucous voices of men. Thrown hastily together, practically overnight, the camp at first glance seemed the mushroom growth it was. It might be innocent, or it might be deadly poison that would kill mercilessly at the slightest taste.

Through the open front door of Kansas Joe's, tough-looking men, dirty and bearded, could be seen standing at the crude bar. Glasses clinked.

'See that side exit, Celestino?' Pryor said quickly to his faithful retainer. 'When the trouble starts, have the horses there and ready, savvy?'

'Yuh expectin' trouble?' asked Billy North.

A slight nod was his reply. Billy North could have left then if he had wished to duck. The Rio Kid appeared to know just what he was doing in Cherryville.

'Okay, General,' Mireles told his partner. 'I am zere.'

The Kid left leather with his springy, much-

26

alive manner, and stepped into Kansas Joe Murphy's. North came right behind him, coonskin tassel brushing his ear and cheek. There were about thirty men in the place. A couple of men who wore guns served drinks, and others were playing cards or throwing dice. The floor was simply trodden dirt, the tables of roughly-planed, round sections of big trees. The bar was made of boards set on thicker chunks of trunks. Logs or wooden boxes served as chairs. Barrels or whiskey on tap were the main refreshment. Hanging from the low log beams lanterns cast a vague, yellow glow.

The Rio Kid paused inside the doorway, his practiced eyes taking in the gathering. Most of them seemed to be Frontier toughs, gunnies carrying smooth-handled Colts in ready holsters, as well as long knives. A few were evidently new arrivals, men from the wagon trains which had paused at Cherryville to outfit.

'Set 'em up,' ordered the Kid, tossing money on the bar.

He kept his face frozen, his eyes slitted, as he gazed about the room. Some of the fellows in Kansas Joe's returned his hard glance, but others did not notice it.

Pryor and North tossed down drinks of the raw red liquor that was drawn from a tap in the half-barrel set on stilts behind the bar.

'*Oof!*' the Kid said in a loud, clear voice.

'Ain't fit for swine, though I reckon it'll do here.'

A sudden silence fell upon the saloon. A man got up from a box, at the rear, where he had been leaning back against the log wall, chinked with mud.

The Rio Kid took him in. He was short and wide, with a wiry black beard, ragged mustache, and long, matted, greasy hair. His ugly face was broad, his nose squashed flat against it. His legs were short for such an immense trunk, and they were bowed to the shape of a horse's ribs.

He was attired in a stained black suit, the pants tucked into muddy halfboots. A once-white shirt was open, showing the hairy chest. On one stubby finger shone a gold ring with a big diamond in it, although the ring did not fit well, looking as though it might have belonged to somebody else at one time.

'So,' he growled, 'yuh don't fancy no likker, Mister?'

He fixed the Rio Kid with small, red-rimmed, shifty eyes.

'Well,' Pryor said frankly, 'I've tasted better every place I ever was. You own this hellhole?'

'Yeah, I do.'

'Then yuh're Kansas Joe Murphy,' Pryor said.

'I might be,' admitted the proprietor coldly.

Billy North had trailed the Kid down the bar, as they met Kansas Joe. Murphy was not yet convinced of the complaining customer's intentions, but he was wary, and his hands were not far from his guns. Murphy's guns were slung in front, tied by rawhide strings above his thick knees.

'What yuh doin' in Cherryville?' Murphy demanded. 'Are yuh huntin' for an outfit, or for trouble. We can accommodate yuh with either.'

Bob Pryor ignored this rough olive branch. He laughed, rather raucously.

'Trouble's my middle name, Murphy.'

Kansas Joe went red but he gulped and muttered:

'Come down here, and I'll set yuh up to a drink.'

The Kid shrugged, and stood at the bar with Murphy, although he kept half turned and always alert, while North watched his back for him.

'Calm yoreself down, feller,' advised Kansas Joe, his voice low. 'If yuh really wanta fight, I can oblige yuh.'

'How so?' snapped the Kid.

'I'll offer yuh a job, if yuh prove yoreself—'

Soupy Griggs came a-tooting into the saloon. He slid to a stop as his ratty eyes took in the Rio Kid and North.

'Hey, hey, Boss!' he shouted, his voice a high-pitched whine. 'Them there polecats jest shot up the store and plugged one of the boys!'

Behind the little storekeeper showed several of the gunnies who had been hanging around the store.

'So that's yore game!' Murphy cried furiously. 'Why, yuh'll be tore to pieces, damn yore hide, bustin' up my town—'

The Kid's hand flickered out like the head of a striking rattler, smacked like a pistol shot against Murphy's bearded cheek.

'Look out!' shrieked Griggs, dancing up and down. 'He's quick as lightnin'!'

CHAPTER IV

Military Mission

Instant fractions ticked away. A gunny in the corner, believing he had a chance to catch the Rio Kid, started out his Colt, his teeth bared in a snarl. With his army pistol flashing like legerdemain, the Kid snapped a bullet at him. The would be killer fell back against the wall, kicking his legs and howling.

'Hold yore guns, gents!' the Kid's icy voice roared. 'I'll drill the next one that tries that between the eyes!'

Tense silence descended on the saloon. Kansas Joe Murphy, his dirty hand itching to go for his guns, was but a step from the man with the determined chin and hard eyes. He dared not start, however. The Kid's shooting was too good.

'What yuh want?' he said thickly, but Pryor reached out, grabbed his arm and swung him around.

With a pistol barrel rammed in his back ribs, Murphy obeyed with alacrity the tense command:

'Elevate!'

His men could not shoot now, even had they wished to buck the Rio Kid, for a slug might strike their boss.

'Back up toward the door,' Pryor ordered.

Hands overhead, licking his thick lips, Kansas Joe Murphy reluctantly covered the Kid's retreat to the side door, while Billy North, gun in hand, and blindly trusting the Rio Kid, hastily went along.

Mireles was on his mustang in the shadows, with Saber and North's gelding ready.

'Get mounted, Billy,' Pryor said coolly.

The bulk of Kansas Joe Murphy filled the narrow side door, as the proprietor faced the lighted saloon. The *Rio Kid* raised his spurred, booted foot, planted it in Murphy's back, and gave a vigorous shove. The kick sent Kansas Joe hurtling into the saloon, off balance. He slid, tripped over a tree stump chair, and fell flat on his ugly face.

Pryor's gun barked twice, rapidly, and two of the lanterns went out, hot glass tinkling down. With a shrill war-whoop, the Rio Kid bounded to Saber's saddle, and they were off, riding around the back of the place and splashing across the ford of Cherry Creek. There the trio hit the dark woods.

'Well, dang my hide!' gasped Billy North, staring back at the lighted camp which was ringing with shouts of roused-up gunnies. 'Since when'd you turn bad man, Kid?'

Captain Pryor reined in the sorrel, and turned the dun, sitting his saddle and watching Cherryville. He did not reply to North's query.

'I'm goin' back and hurrah the town,' he said instead. 'You can come with me or not, as yuh like, Billy.'

North shook his puzzled head. However, he was not the kind to quit a comrade.

'Guns out,' ordered the Kid. 'But don't kill anybody 'less they try to take us, and be careful of them immigrant folks.'

The three spurred back, picking up to full speed, low over the saddle, and straight along the rutted single road of the camp. Whooping like Indians, they fired their pistols, smacking bullets high into the faces of the buildings. Flying as madly as centaurs, they 'hurrahed' the camp, and the slugs that were hastily thrown at the shadowy, hard-riding three only sang whistling threats about them as they sped on.

But Kansas Joe Murphy, insulted to the core of his soul, furious at the insolent hurrahing of his camp, was roaring commands. Armed hombres were running to the saloon from all directions, grabbing horses, and collecting at their chief's order.

The Kid yanked the swift dun to a sliding stop, whirled and then started back down the road. Mireles and North were at Saber's flying heels.

Bullets kept the gunnies ducking, but as the Kid and his mates reached the end of the line of crude hovels, Murphy's fighting men came sweeping forth in hot pursuit.

'Keep out in front, now!' shouted Pryor. 'We'll lead 'em a sweet run for their money.'

Kansas Joe, smarting for revenge, rode among his killers. There were several dozen of them about the bearded, bow-legged devil who ran Cherryville. Splashing again over Cherry Creek, the Rio Kid took the rear guard, and his Colts flashed back, singing bullets over the pursuers.

There was a horse trail that Mireles chose, evidently knowing it. North was aware of that trail, too, for he had come up from the southwest that way. Along this they kept racing, although the Kid never got too far in front of their pursuers to discourage Kansas Joe from the chase.

For miles the Kid held Kansas Joe Murphy, leading him on with most of his band. The horses were lathered, and the soft breeze of the wilds was in their faces, whipping their hats as they rode.

'I reckon they'll be droppin' us soon,' panted Pryor, looking back.

The gunmen were strung out for a long distance behind. Kansas Joe was plainly tiring of the attempt to catch up with the fast-running mounts of the three who had offered such an indignity to Cherryville.

Soon after, they heard shouts from the pursuers. Murphy's riders pulled up, fired an ineffectual volley, and then swung, starting back for Cherryville.

The Kid pulled up, too, and began to roll a smoke. His infectious grin, reckless and merry under any odds, even in the face of death, flashed at Billy North who shook his head.

'I still don't savvy,' the buffalo hunter growled. 'Why risk yore neck jest for fun?'

'Had a good reason for it all, Billy,' the Kid told him. 'Yuh'll soon learn if yuh stick with me. But I reckon now a little shut-eye would do us all good.'

The Kid knew how to camp in hostile country and so did North. They realized how happy Kansas Joe's gang would be to come upon them asleep, and there were always bands of raiding Indians wandering around ready to slit anybody's throat for his horses and other possessions.

The animals were turned loose. Saber was allowed to roam free, for he would come at the Kid's call. The other two horses were hobbled. Carrying saddles and bedrolls, the men walked up to a woods where they hid themselves and slept, wrapped against the coolness, head on leather . . .

Pryor was up with the first streak of dawn and waked his companions. They ate cold jerked venison and hardtack, washed down with clear water from a spring.

The Rio Kid, a trained wilderness scout who had had plenty of experience in enemy territory while he had done such work for General Custer during the Civil War, went up and surveyed the horizons.

The dun was grazing not far away, and the Kid approached his pet, softly singing:

Said the big black charger to the little white
    mare,
The sergeant claims yore feed bill really
    ain't fair.

It was an old army song and had a thousand or more verses. The lanky dun loved it and always responded to it, whether it was whistled, sung or played on a bugle. It soothed his wild mustang heart. Now he sniffed at the Kid's hand as the wiry Pryor leaped to his back and rode to saddle up and fetch the other mounts.

Saber was a fighter, too. He would run to battle if allowed. He enjoyed the fray, the scent of powder-smoke. He had carried the Kid through dangerous runs in the war, and afterward on the Frontier from the Rio to Dakota.

With Celestino Mireles, lean and silent, his deep-set eyes and arrogant nose shaded by his peaked Mexican sombrero, and Billy North, young and strong, Bob Pryor headed northeast. He kept to an Indian trail through an arroyo that sheltered them from chance spying eyes.

After they had rapidly traveled this faint trail for a couple of hours, the Kid caught the call of a quail, repeated twice. He reined in, and Billy North, listening to what went on now, finally had an explanation of Pryor's strange behavior of the previous night.

A man awaited the Kid, hidden from sight or hearing of any hostiles. It was he who had whistled the perfectly simulater quail notes, signaling Pryor.

'Who's that stranger with yuh?' the waiting man asked from his thicket.

'Billy North, a man to ride the river with,' replied the Kid.

'All right. C'mon in.'

Magically the thicket parted and the three passed through, leading their animals, into a shaded grove of oaks.

The man who had stopped them was around thirty, about five-feet-eight, heavy-set, with stooping shoulders and a ragged dark mustache above his determined mouth. He wore buckskin, and his hunter's hat was hanging from his belt, where his pistols rode. Scout moccasins were on his feet. A Sharps rifle was leaning against a nearby tree and to the rear was hobbled a chestnut horse, muzzled by a bandanna.

His clear, dark-blue eyes fixed the three.

'Meet Charlie Reynolds,' the Rio Kid said, introducing the young hunter.

North's face lighted up.

'Powerful pleased, Reynolds,' he exclaimed. 'I've heard tell of yuh!'

The debonair Kid squatted beside the great scout.

'Charlie's sorta nosed me out with Custer since the War,' he remarked. 'He's the General's favorite now, shore enough. And the best shot in the West, bar none.'

'Lonesome Charlie' Reynolds, as he was called, the best hunter on the Frontier, and a great scout, paid no heed to the Kid's compliments.

'Did it work?' the Kid asked him curiously.

'Shore,' Reynolds told him. 'Fine, Kid.' The brooding dark-blue eyes scanned the faces of the three who had come up. 'Thanks.'

'It's quite a set-up Kansas Joe's got there,' the Kid went on. 'Big gang of gunnies, if ever I saw any, ridin' for him. They're outfittin' parties hand over fist to go into the Hills. The General's hunch was right.'

'Uh-huh.' Reynolds nodded.

'Have any trouble gettin' in that warehouse,

37

after we led 'em off last night?' inquired Pryor.

'Nope. Hull bunch went after yuh, Kid.'

Billy North saw the light then.

'So yuh done it a-purpose, to give Reynolds a chance to get in!' he exclaimed. 'Now I savvy. ' 'Twasn't like you to hurrah a town jest for the fun of it.'

'There's been a bunch of killin's laid to the Sioux in the Black Hills, North,' Bob Pryor explained. 'folks like that party with the young lady yuh're so interested in. General Custer wanted to know about them killin's, and he also wanted to trace a leak in military supplies for garrisons on the upper Missouri. Reckon we've found it. Don't you think so, Charlie?'

'Reckon so,' Lonesome Charlie replied.

Reynolds was a man of few words.

'Kansas Joe Murphy's gettin' them supplies,' went on the Kid. 'He sells cheap since he pays nothin' for 'em.'

'Marked "condemned",' growled Reynolds.

'The old army game,' Pryor declared.

'Soupy Lou Griggs got mighty sore when I warned Burton not to enter the Black Hills,' North informed the great scout. 'That wagon train was made up in Yankton on the Missouri, but they come here to stock up.'

'Shore,' grunted the Kid. 'It's plain enough. Murphy and Griggs got steerers in the towns who egg pioneers into the Hills, and send 'em to Cherryville to buy supplies. They're cleanin' up plenty. It'll drive the Sioux to war.'

'Somethin' has got to be done to save Burton's party, boys,' declared North.

'Yuh're right,' the Rio Kid firmly agreed. 'If a big bunch like that is massacred it'll rouse the whole nation. Me, I feel like Custer does. I'm sorry for the Sioux, and the Hills're theirs. Reynolds, s'pose we cut south of Cherry Crik and make for the Hills. Custer told us to take a look-see there. In a day or two, when them immigrants are outa the way of Kansas Joe's gang and town, we'll head up and chase Burton back.'

'All right,' said Charlie Reynolds.

The four swung off south.

The Rio Kid was well aware of the tense situation in Dakota, of the pressure and conflict between whites and reds. Sitting Bull, medicine man of the Sioux, and fast becoming their chief leader, had sent warnings to the Fort, warnings that the Sioux would not give up the Black Hills.

Now, backed by General George Armstrong Custer, the Rio Kid sought to save the land from bloody war.

CHAPTER V

Escape

All day, the Rio Kid and his companions rode, then camped, cunningly, hidden at night. Cherryville lay to the northeast. The rising Black Hills were before them.

The Kid and Reynolds were out ahead, North and Mireles in the rear. Suddenly, Saber sniffed and reared, and the Kid swung in his leather. On the faint trail they were following lay a dead man, his head a horror.

'Lost his hair,' the Kid growled.

The two scouts were down, hunting sign. The dead white man's pack and animals were missing. Everything was gone except the rough clothing in which he had died.

Billy North and Mireles pushed up, staring at the scalped victim.

'The Sioux!' North growled at first glance.

'Huh!' grunted the Rio Kid, exchanging glances with Reynolds. 'Tracks are two days old. That thunder shower washed 'em out some. But—it ain't jest right. What you figger, Reynolds?'

Lonesome Charlie shrugged.

'Looks like we better get after that bunch North is so interested in.'

'That's what I'm thinkin',' agreed the Kid.

'Let's ride.'

They shoved northward. Because of the Rio Kid's scouting genius and Reynolds' great ability, they were always alert, ever-daring, but with the cunning of savages. Only in such manner could a white man hope to keep his hair on for long in that land.

As it grew nearer to night, the Rio Kid, out in front on Saber, came onto the wider track of a wagon train. The sun was red over the mighty summits of the Black Hills, but still there was not much light left. Such a trail, however, might be followed in the darkness by an expert.

Pryor read that it had been several hours since the train had gone by, but superimposed on its sign were hundreds of hoofprints much fresher. These puzzled him, and he consulted Charlie Reynolds as the scout and hunter came up.

'Look!' the Kid said, and picked up a stained eagle feather. 'But some of them mustangs are shod, Reynolds, and Indian mustangs ain't. And comin' from this direction—'

'What is it?' asked North, swinging from his leather.

'Yore friends' trail. And a big party of riders on it.'

The quartet pressed on, as darkness dropped over the mysterious wilderness like a velvet cloak. Stars sprang up in the sky dome,

41

while a half moon lent a sickly yellow light to the scene.

The dun ran with a hare's fleetness. Wind rushed past his rider's bronzed, handsome face, grim in the shadow of the Stetson. Up onto a rise went the horse, and the Rio Kid's keen eyes sought the wide, wooded depression. A great shallow valley swept for miles before him, clogged by forests, dense bush and bizarre rock shapes, while in the center of it meandered a stream, its banks choked with growth.

The breeze brought the odor of burning wood to the Kid's flared nostrils and his glance swept the spaces ahead.

'Camped down there, in the hollow by the crik,' he muttered.

A horse whinnied suddenly to the right, a neigh cut short as though muffled. Pryor swung off the dun, as Reynolds and North, trailed by Mireles, shoved up and paused on the ridge.

'Wait'll I check that,' whispered the Rio Kid.

Like a wraith in the night he started along the west slope of the valley, and in a short time heard the soft rustle of many hoofs in the grass. A large number of horses were being watched by silent, half-naked figures in the woods.

Pryor snaked away, back to his comrades.

'No time to lose,' he told them. 'They're

already circlin'. C'mon—we'll try to bust it up real quick!'

Leaping on Saber, he cut down the wagon trail broken by Burton's party. His voice rose, shrill and startling in the night, a Rebel yell that rang for miles in the Hills, a warning to the pioneers below.

Now he glimpsed the red glow of fire coals, and as he heard shrieks and howls banging in the darkness, firearms began blazing in the valley. A circle of men with guns had crept upon the wagon caravan, and the Kid's warning had rushed their attack.

The Rio Kid, Colts out, guiding the dun with his knees, rode toward the lines of painted, naked savages that sprang up around the Burton camp. Ahead he could see the dim shapes of the wagons. Then the glowing coals of the immigrants' fire were doused, as the men, warned by the Kid's shouts, sprang to their rifles for defense.

A befeathered head, turning on him, and the glint of gun metal, started Bob Pryor's pistols roaring. The Indian crashed over, and the Kid turned the dun, full-tilt, along the line, smashing through low brush and rounding heaps of stones.

Reynolds, North and Mireles were after him, their weapons blazing. They folded the line of attackers up, creating terrific confusion. Deadly Colts spat and tore at the surprised ambushers, caught in the same sort of trap they had set themselves.

From the direction of the camp, heavy Sharps buffalo guns began to blast, as a gang of redmen to the right rushed toward the wagons, shooting as they plunged forward.

Hot and fierce the battle rose, the Kid fighting with a silent fury to disorganize the foe.

A slug bit a chunk of flesh from his left arm, stung him frightfully. Another cut a hole in his hat brim. He heard Billy North give a startled, amazed curse, then was aware that North had hurtled from his saddle.

Whipping to a stop, the Kid pivoted on a dime. Reynolds and Mireles had swung, guns blasting at a bunch of naked Indians, faces dark with streaks of paint, heads feathered, running in to finish North.

The Kid hit dirt, bent over his prostrate friend. Billy North seemed dead. Blood was on his face, and his head was as limp as an old rag doll's as the Rio Kid threw him across the back of Celestino's horse.

'Ride back and head on east, pronto,' snapped the Kid, and the Mexican youth obeyed, used to following his leader's orders.

Reynolds' dangerous guns held back the enraged Indians as the Kid leaped on Saber. The two scouts, hard-pressed as the infuriated enemies turned upon them, were forced into the woods by charging redmen, yelling in high-pitched voices and throwing hot lead at them.

The deep-throated roars of Sharps, the whipping of Winchesters, barking Colts, dominated the valley. No longer did it brood with peace, but was a noisy inferno because of the hatred of struggling men. With Billy North and Mireles gone, only Reynolds and the Kid remained to aid the Burton people. But they had given warning, and the pioneers were roused, and shooting from behind their wagons.

'Let's get back and stampede them Injun hosses,' the Kid told Charlie Reynolds.

Reynolds, cool as a cucumber, never got excited when in danger. He accepted the Kid's suggestion and they fought back over their shoulders as they slowly retreated.

Mounted, they could travel faster than their adversaries. They curved north along a bushy slope for the woods where the Kid had smelled out the mustangs. They reached the hidden clearing well out in front of pursuers.

Guns banging, whooping it up, Reynolds and the Kid spurred in among the animals. Half a dozen buckskin-clad, painted and feathered figures bellowed at them, sought to bring them down with blazing pistols.

'Let 'em have it, Charlie!' roared Pryor, his own pistols blazing.

The two scouts hit four of the six horse guards within half a minute and the remaining ones, appalled at the slaughter, dropped the bridles they held and scuttled off into the

45

trees.

It was then a cinch to complete the rout of the enemy mounts. There were seventy of them, and most were saddled. Saber bit and kicked, helping to create confusion that turned the orderly ranks into a milling hell.

'Run 'em over the ridge!' bawled the Rio Kid, as dust rolled up from drumming hoofs.

They had most of the animals headed east, as the enemy van appeared on their trail along the ridge, shooting and yelling at them.

Lead sang about them, but they rapidly left the gang of confused swearing redmen behind. The mustangs ran like mad before them, and after a mile, began splitting off in bunches to the sides.

The Rio Kid, bleeding from flesh wounds, throat full of dust and dry from the battle, slowed the dun. Charlie Reynolds rode up to his side.

'That oughta put a crimp in their plans, for tonight, anyways,' Pryor growled. 'What do you think, Charlie?'

Lonesome Charlie Reynolds grunted. 'Reckon yuh're right, Kid. If that fool bunch of immigrants don't take warnin' from this and skedaddle, it ain't our hard luck.'

'They got hosses and can run for it,' said the Rio Kid. 'As I see it, since we've given those folks their chance to escape, it's up to us to report to Custer pronto, on what we've found out.'

Charlie Reynolds nodded. 'We head for the Fort, Kid.'

To the west only scattered firing came, dimly, on the wind. They had thrown a wrench into the intended massacre of Burton's people, offered the pioneers life instead of death. Now duty called, and the two could do no more against the large gang they had run upon.

Besides, Pryor was worried about North.

'Wait'll I rope a spare mustang,' he said.

He caught up with a straggler, a chestnut mare with a saddle askew on her back, and tossed his lariat loop easily over her neck, stopping her.

The two comrades set their horses east, leading the mare, galloping full tilt to overtake Mireles.

In an hour they came up with the Mexican. The lad's animal, carrying double, could not travel fast.

Pausing to give first aid to the still unconscious Billy North, the Kid and Charlie Reynolds found that a deep crease had been made by a .45 slug in North's scalp. Blood, oozing out, had matted his light hair and dried on his cheeks.

'Breathin's ragged,' growled the Kid. 'He's got a little concussion, I reckon.'

His busy fingers tore strips from North's shirt-tail, and he made a rough bandage.

47

CHAPTER VI

Sun Dance Torture

Fastened to the mare's back, Billy North rode as comfortably as they could make it. They bore northeast, off the wagon trail, and cut several miles west of Cherryville, crossing Cherry Creek.

By dawn they were well to the northwest of the camp of Kansas Joe Murphy. Only then did they pause, by a little rill off the winding trail that finally led to the upper reaches of the Missouri and Fort Abraham Lincoln.

As they laid him out on a blanket spread on the grass of the small clearing in the woods, Billy North's handsome face was pale as flour under his sun tan.

The Rio Kid sighed.

'He can never stand a long ride—not for a couple days, anyway,' pronounced Bob Pryor. 'One of us'll have to stick here with him.'

'I do eet, General,' Celestino offered.

'He'll need careful nursin',' observed Reynolds, squatted on his haunches, and tearing chunks from a strip of deer meat with his even, white teeth.

The Kid washed the young hunter's head wound with clear water from the brook and poured some between the lax lips. North

48

stirred and grunted, but when his eyes opened it was plain that his brain was still stunned. He did not recognize his friends, and sought to fight them, although he was too weak to move. 'Someone comin' down the trail!' exclaimed Pryor. 'Wait! I'll see who it is.'

He stole out, crouched low by the side of the winding trail. The sounds of creaking leather, the faint thud of hoofs on the ground had warned his keen ears of this approach.

A figure in buckskin, mounted on a dapple-gray horse, and trailed by two pack-horses loaded high with bales, came slowly around the bend into the Kid's range of vision.

At first look, Pryor thought it was a man, for the clothing was masculine, and a rifle rode the crook of the stranger's bent arm, as watchful eyes flitted from left to right for signs of danger in the wilds.

But Bob Pryor was acquainted with most of the Frontier characters of his time. He knew their habit of wandering from one camp to another as each had its heyday and a new one sprang into popularity.

'By hell!' he cried, jumping up. 'It's Calamity Jane!'

The rifle flew up, covering him. Then the muzzle dropped, and white teeth flashed a smile at the handsome Kid.

'Howdy, Rio Kid!'

'Howdy, Calamity. What you doin' in these parts?'

49

It was a woman who faced the Rio Kid. At maturity, Martha Jane Canary, nicknamed 'Calamity Jane' on the Frontier, was solid and graceful of body, wholesome and good-looking. She was of medium height, and dark-brown hair peeped from under her beaver hat, trimmed with a red feather. Her large brown eyes fixed the Kid.

Pryor knew that her skill with a rifle and six-gun equalled that of most men of the west. She was as good a hunter as any man, except the most expert scouts. She had driven a mail coach, punched cows, hunted outlaws, and was a welcome figure anywhere, for it was said she came in mighty handy in times of calamity.

'I'm headin' for that new camp of Cherryville,' Calamity Jane informed Pryor. 'Got a stock of trade goods and aim to turn over a little profit, Kid.'

'If yuh're as smart as I know yuh are, Calamity,' the Kid said, 'yuh'll steer clear of that camp. It's run by an outlaw gang. The head's Kansas Joe Murphy.'

'Dawggone it! Joe Murphy, hey? Why, he's been chased by more vigilantes than any other bandit in Dakota . . . You all alone?'

'Nope. Charlie Reynolds and my pardner, Celestino Mireles, along with a young hunter, Billy North, who's hurt right bad, are near here, Calamity. C'mon and have a bite with us.'

The Rio Kid led Martha Jane Canary

through to the hidden clearing. She greeted Reynolds and the Mexican calmly, as man to man. Then she caught the sight of the wounded North, pale and gasping on the blanket.

Her woman's heart was touched, and she quickly knelt by North's head.

'He's hurt bad,' she said. 'You fellows oughta know that. Why, he's got a concussion or I'm a prairie dog! He's got to be kept quiet and nursed careful.'

Taking charge with speedy efficiency, Calamity Jane forgot her own business and settled down to heating water and steaming cloths clean.

'Got some tea with me,' she announced. 'That's what he needs.'

'Reynolds and me got to be ridin',' the Kid told her, when she had finished cleaning up and bandaging Billy North's head in a manner that satisfied her. 'We meant to leave Mireles here with North. Yuh reckon you could stay, Calamity? Celestino can do the huntin' for yuh and cut wood, and stand guard.'

'Shore, shore. I wouldn't leave this poor hombre to men's mercies now, Kid.'

'Fine. Then we'll be back when we're back. When North's all right, tell him we'll pick him up here.'

Saddling up, the two scouts said *adios*, and swung on the long run north to Fort Abraham Lincoln, where General George Armstrong

Custer awaited their report.

They rode all day, ever on the alert. Near evening, the Kid raised his hand, and both scouts got down to view the fresh trail they had come upon, cutting in from the southwest wilderness.

The Kid drew the side of his hand across his throat.

'Sioux!' he grunted, and Lonesome Charlie nodded.

'They ain't on the warpath, though,' Reynolds observed.

They kept on, but more slowly. They knew now that a couple of hundred Indians rode ahead of them, and knowing the ferocity of the Sioux, for whom the sign language of all tribes was cutthroat, as the Kid had gestured, the two were not desirous of running on the redmen's heels without due warning.

'There's goin' to be war with the Sioux 'fore long,' Pryor predicted. 'And it's goin' to be a tough one. Yuh hear 'em complainin' constant about the transcontinental railroad that cuts their huntin' grounds in half. The buffalo are gettin' scarcer, their game is most gone, and if the Black Hills are taken from 'em, that'll be the last straw.'

'Right,' agreed Reynolds. 'And it'll be some war, Kid!'

They rode after the night fell, but when the moon came up, they camped off the trail for sleep. In the morning they were again on their way, pushing toward Fort Abraham Lincoln. In the middle of the sunny afternoon weird sounds, the *rub-a-dub-dub* of Indian drums, and blood-curdling shrieks could be heard from west of the path they were following.

'Let's see what they're up to,' Lonesome Charlie suggested. 'Custer'll wanta know.'

The scouts dismounted and pulled off their boots, replacing them with soft moccasins. They left hats and creaking leather behind with their horses, and stole, silent as panthers, for a peek at the Sioux.

In a forest clearing fires for cooking blazed high. Spits with deer meat joints were turned by squaws before the coals, and the smell of cooking venison was in the warm air.

Leaping figures were howling in a circle around poles arranged in the center. They were awesome in their elaborate beaded buckskin and white fur tippets and with eagle feathers banded about the black straight hair above their painted faces.

A huge Sioux, naked save for a breech-clout, and with face and hair matted by sweat, hung suspended from the set-up of poles.

Incisions had been made in the flesh on both sides of the tortured Indian's chest. Rawhide strips had been shoved through and tied to the tendons, so that his full weight was supported on them. Blood flowed down to his belly, as the Indian plunged and kicked his feet, the thongs ripping at his ligaments. He must either tear entirely loose, without showing any pain whatever, or keep it up until he fainted. If he failed to break the tendons or struggle until he was finished, then he was branded a coward. Sometimes this took two or three days and nights of torture dancing.

'Sun dance!' whispered Reynolds to Pryor.

'Huh! They ain't painted for war, anyway. Say, there's Sitting Bull!'

'Right.'

Reynolds could speak the Sioux tongue and Pryor knew a good many words of the Indian language. A lean, fierce Sioux, breast scarred showing he had undergone the sun dance torture, leaped to the fore.

'I, Spotted Fawn, have killed the white men!' he shouted over the din. 'I, Spotted Fawn will kill the *wasichus*, our white foes, until the sun no longer burns! The *wasichus* have slaughtered our buffalo and cut our hunting grounds in two. Now they seek to steal from us the sacred Hills. On the creek called French I have taken the scalps of eight invaders of our lands. We must fight, kill until no more *wasichus* come toward the sunset!'

'That Spotted Fawn,' remarked Reynolds, 'is a bad Indian if ever there was one. Reckon he's been busy scalpin' and killin' in the Black Hills, Kid. Listen to him. Now he's sayin' he knows where the Sioux can get better guns than Pahuska's soldiers have, and backin' from white men who hate their own kind!'

'Pahuska'—Long Hair—was the Sioux nickname for General Custer, the Kid knew. Spotted Fawn raved on, speaking that name and others, shrieking his words at the circle of braves.

'He's got a Great Chief, he says,' translated Reynolds, 'who's white who will help the Sioux regain their rights.'

After a time Spotted Fawn quieted down, and other savages began boasting and proclaiming their exploits.

'Let's get our hosses and visit 'em,' suggested Pryor. 'Yeah, we better. Sittin' Bull loves a spiel.'

They were not more than half a day's run from the Fort on the upper Missouri. The Sioux evidently were headed for the army post themselves, and would not be liable to attack the scouts, since they were nowhere near the reservation.

The two scouts stole away. Resuming their hats and boots and leather, they rode openly along the trail into the Sioux camp.

Wild shrieks arose on the air at sight of the whites. Spotted Fawn and a dozen warriors, waving hatchets and rifles, dashed toward them, but neither scout showed any perturbation or took notice. They went up to Sitting Bull and dismounted beside the famous medicine man, leader of the Sioux.

'How,' the Kid greeted, echoed by Reynolds.

'Ugh! How, *wasichu* scouts. How, The-Hunter-Who-Never-Goes-Out-for-Nothing!' Sitting Bull glanced for a moment at Bob Pryor, and added: 'How, The-Man-Who-Rides-Like-The-Wind!'

Sitting Bull was nearing forty. He was of middle height, inclined to stoutness, and his hair was short for a Sioux. He had the typical oval, high-boned face and curving nose of the Dakota Indian. All in all, his demeanor was forbidding, but he concealed his ferocity under an air of good humor.

The Rio Kid had met Sitting Bull the year before at a Kansas settlement. At that time, there had been some horse races and Saber had outrun the best mustangs of Indians and cowboys. Sitting Bull recalled this occasion and from it bestowed on Bob Pryor a Sioux title describing his outstanding achievement in Indian eyes.

After greetings and smoking, Sitting Bull began to question Reynolds on hunting. It was a sore point with the Sioux that Reynolds would not tell them the magic by which he brought home so much game. As a medicine man, Sitting Bull desired the secret.

The Kid, squatted beside Sitting Bull and Reynolds, listened to the talk. He was aware that Spotted Fawn's evil, burning eyes were fixed upon him every instant, filled with a black hate.

'Seems to savvy us,' he thought. 'Wonder

who his white chief could be? Mebbe Kansas Joe Murphy!'

Reynolds parried Sitting Bull's questions about the hunting medicine, but no denials that his skill did not come from unearthly power could convince the Sioux. The heavy-set chief grew irritated, in fact, because Lonesome Charlie would not give formulas for blessing a gun with which to bring down game.

Reynolds finally managed to switch the topic of conversation to the presence of the Indians in these parts.

'We go to the Fort,' replied Sitting Bull. 'Pahuska, Long Hair, must listen to us. The Sioux are starving and we want food.'

Surrounded by the ferocious redmen, the scouts calmly partook of venison strips and smoked.

Spotted Fawn, the Kid noted from the corner of a veiled blue eye, was edging closer and closer to Charlie Reynolds. Pryor, on his haunches, tensed. He could not see Spotted Fawn's right hand, but Lonesome Charlie was engrossed in his spiel with Sitting Bull, and Spotted Fawn made no sounds.

Suddenly the Kid shoved hard from his squatting posture, and caught Spotted Fawn's descending arm. In the savage's strong hand a long knife was clutched, aimed at Reynolds' back ribs.

It was so close that the knife grazed

Charlie's leather, cut a slit in the jacket. Then the Kid's weight turned the murderous thrust, and he ripped Spotted Fawn's wrist up behind his back.

'Drop that knife, Spotted Fawn!' he cried.

CHAPTER VII

Army Post

Like holding a giant snake it was to hold Spotted Fawn who, lithe and powerful, sought to eel from the steel grip of the Rio Kid. Pryor's leg swept against Spotted Fawn's shins, throwing him farther off balance, and the twisted arm bones of the Sioux could no longer withstand the skillful pressure Bob Pryor applied.

The long scalping knife, sharp as a razor, flashed as it fell from Spotted Fawn's fingers. And the Kid, aware that this savage was his enemy until death, from now on if not before, put a foot in Spotted Fawn's back and shoved hard.

The Sioux hit dirt, and rolled, over and over, coming up on his feet several yards from the Kid, fury glinting in his dark eyes.

A tense silence was upon the gathering. Death was upon the two scouts, depending on how the Sioux took the Kid's necessary play.

Pryor stood still, hands easy at his sides, close to his six-shooters. His face was set, but his eyes were glinting.

Sitting Bull, seeing the knife, the thrust at Reynolds frustrated by Bob Pryor's quick action, suddenly frowned at Spotted Fawn, but his broad face twitched in a smile at Bob Pryor.

'Now your name is changed, Man-Who-Rides-Like-The-Wind,' Sitting Bull remarked in a clear voice. 'It shall be Man-Quick-As-Lightning.' And without looking at Spotted Fawn again, Sitting Bull added: 'Perhaps those who Spotted Fawn, the Warrior-Who-Drops-His-Knife, claim lie in the Black Hills were women and children. They could never have been men! I will deal later with him who violates the hospitality of Sitting Bull.'

Derisive glances were cast at Spotted Fawn by his Indian companions. The chief's withering remark and the threat of punishment crushed him. He had struck and had ignominiously missed, been disarmed. Swinging, he stalked to his mustang, leaped on, and rode away.

Both scouts relaxed. They could have taken a dozen Sioux with them to death, but now a finish fight was not forced.

However, they thought it best to leave the Indians. The big brave was still kicking and plunging, suspended from the poles. Declining Sitting Bull's invitation to ride to the Fort with

59

the Sioux next day, the scouts mounted and swung on north.

'Much obliged, Kid,' Reynolds said. 'That Spotted Fawn's a bad customer.'

'Reckon we'll tangle with him again. Like to meet the white man who's backin' him!'

'So would Custer.'

They rode on swiftly, and camped after midnight. On the flat Dakota plains, swept by every wind, they rolled in blankets under the stars. And in the morning they trotted their horses up to Fort Abraham Lincoln where the muddy Missouri rolled to the east.

Smoke curled up from cook fires and rose lazily toward the long chain of bluffs behind the post. Soldiers were busy in the enclosure. A sentry challenged them, recognized the scouts, and passed them.

There were women around, and Indians stalking about—Indians friendly to the whites, and reservation savages. Everything was bustling activity.

Fort Lincoln was a ten-company post. A wide, gracious plain extended from sheltering hills down to the river bank and on this, in a great square, the buildings stood. Built of native timber as they were, unseasoned cottonwood that shrank as it dried, leaving cracks in the walls, attempts had been made to brighten the structures by painting them white with green trim.

And General Custer's wife, Elizabeth,

better known as 'Libby' to her friends, had planted flowers and had trees set out on the bare spaces.

Little stone lookouts peeped from the distant bluff tops where watchful eyes kept a look-out for raiding parties of Indians, a common affair.

'Seems like Custer's makin' ready to march,' observed the Kid.

'Uh-huh. Shore does.'

Dismounting at the stables, the scouts saw to their horses, then they crossed toward Custer's quarters.

An orderly told them the General was in conference with his staff. Custer sent out word they were to wait, and they hung around in the hall.

A door at the back opened and a slim, pretty young woman came out. When she saw the two, she smiled and walked lightly toward them.

'Captain Pryor! Mr. Reynolds! How do you do?'

Bob Pryor had met the gracious Libby Custer, the general's wife before. Everybody loved her. Although brought up in a sheltered civilization with every luxury, she had chosen to follow her husband to the rough Frontier, where dangers besieged her on every hand.

'Howdy, ma'am,' the Kid greeted, smiling.

Through the door he could see the living room, furnished with a piano, bits of favorite belongings brought the long route from the East, a chair or two, a divan, pieces of family silver. Over a huge stone fireplace were heads of bighorn sheep and antelope, and in the center a buffalo bull, for Custer was a great hunter. The floor was covered by animal pelts for rugs.

The house showed the woman's touch, for wherever Libby Custer went, in tent or Frontier outpost or on a visit to the East, she made a home for her husband. The long days of anxious waiting when he was swallowed up in the wilds, on campaign when she could not go with him, were torture to her.

While the Kid and Reynolds, were talking with Mrs. Custer, the orderly came back and told them that the general would see them.

The lion-maned Custer sat at his desk in his square office. To know George Armstrong Custer was never to forget him, and the Kid had ridden under him through the Civil War, on his staff as a scout and courier. Custer had a hip-hip-hooray way of doing things, and his picturesque uniforms, designed by himself, as well as his yellow mane that hung to his shoulders, had often startled official Washington.

The general seemed in a good humor now, for he liked to be up and doing, and evidently something was going to happen. Where danger stalked, there rode Custer.

'Howdy, General!' cried the Kid.

Lonesome Charlie Reynolds fixed his deep-set eyes on his chief who held all his loyalty.

'Good morning, Pryor—hello, Reynolds,' said Custer.

There were half a dozen officers in the room; a major, two captains, lieutenants. The Kid had met them on his previous visit to the post, and greeted them by name.

'Major Clyde—Cap'n Winters—Lieutenant Green—'

The precise Major Hanson Clyde nodded as he bent his dark, massive head over some rough maps.

The burly Captain Winters, his forehead knitted in sullen face, was busily checking long lists. He did not look up, merely grunting a greeting to the Kid and Reynolds.

'Could we speak to yuh alone, General?' asked Pryor.

Custer nodded. Instead of ordering his staff out, he stood up himself, long legs cased in fine cavalry boots with short silver spurs, and strode from the office, the scouts at his heels.

'What is it, boys?' he asked curiously. 'You've finished the investigation I ordered?'

'Yes, sur,' Charlie Reynolds said. 'We run onto plenty.'

'An owlhooter, Kansas Joe Murphy—yuh've prob'ly heard of him,' the Rio Kid explained quickly, his voice so low that only Custer and Charlie heard, 'has set up this Cherryville camp on the edge of the Black Hills, General.

He's got near a hundred gunnies ridin' for him. Reynolds got in at night while I led 'em off on a wild-goose chase, and a lot of yore missin' army stores are in a warehouse behind a store that's run by a feller called Soupy Lou Griggs, who's a pardner of Murphy's. They're steerin' whites into the Hills and sellin' 'em outfits at Cherryville.'

Red blood surged up in Custer's strong, handsome face. His mustache twitched.

'I'll have Murphy's hide for this,' he snapped. 'Nice work, boys. The Black Hills belong to the Sioux, and if I have anything to say about it, they'll stay that way. It'll mean full war if they're taken from the Indians.'

'That's right, General,' agreed the Kid. 'We met Sittin' Bull on his way to the Fort last night. He's gettin' riled. And that ain't all. A big party of pioneers under a feller named Jake Burton done outfitted at Cherryville, and headed into the Black Hills. We come along jest in time to keep 'em from bein' massacred. There were forty or so men, women and children in Burton's bunch.'

'Such a massacre would blow up the whole country,' declared Custer. 'Did the Sioux attack Burton's camp?'

'That's the puzzle, General. Them riders was mostly whites, fixed up as Indians! The sign, their voices, proved it. If yuh want my idea, it was Kansas Joe Murphy's gang, painted and feathered like Sioux. First they

64

sell people stolen army goods, then trail 'em and kill 'em. Up to now it's been small parties that hit for the Hills, two or three men at a time. Burton's is the first big attempt by settlers, but there'll be more. I figger, from what I overheard a bad Indian named Spotted Fawn claim at Sittin' Bull's camp, that some sorta deep game is bein' played. Spotted Fawn spoke of a great Chief, a white man, wishin' to "help" the Sioux. I ain't shore what the stake is and jest what this game is, but I aim to root it all out.'

Custer was furious—furious at the murderous perfidy reported by the Rio Kid and Lonesome Charlie. The general was a man of action, and he would take it, swiftly. His eyes flashed blue sparks, his teeth gritted behind his tawny mustache.

'Yes,' he repeated, 'I'll nail this Kansas Joe Murphy's hide to the post stockade!' Then, more calmly: 'You say you saved Burton's party? Did you run them out of the Hills?'

'No, General. ' 'Twas impossible. Night was on us and we faced scores of gunnies. We lost a man and had to run for it, but we stampeded the enemy's horses and give Burton a chance to escape.'

'Good. As you know, my expedition to the Hills will march within a short time. But we can't wait for such a slow force to reach Cherryville. Come inside, boys.'

Custer swung on his spurred heels, striding

into the office. 'Gentlemen,' he said to his staff, 'I have orders. Captain Winters, you are relieved of your immediate duties.'

Winters started at that, licked his lip. He was alarmed at Custer's abrupt manner. But as the general went on, he grew more at ease, and listened eagerly.

'You will take Troops E and G,' Custer ordered, 'and proceed south to the new settlement on Cherry Creek called Cherryville, at forced march. There you will seize all men in the camp, confiscate all stores, and burn the buildings. Captain Pryor will guide you and act as your chief scout. Take six Ree assistants, Pryor. When you have accomplished this, Captain Winters, you will go into camp and prevent any further encroachment of whites from that point to the Black Hills, and I will connect with your force as soon as possible.'

Captain Frank Winters sprang to his feet, clicked his heels, saluted. His brown eyes flashed, and his face grew suddenly firmer, determined.

'Thank you, sir!' he cried.

About-facing, Winters hurried from the general's office.

The other officers looked enviously about the burly captain. Garrison life was boring and action was most welcome.

Major Hanson Clyde, Lieutenant Green, and others looked appealingly at Custer. All wished to go out on such a foray.

Custer resumed his seat.

'Now, Major Clyde, we'll put the finishing touches on this. Lieutenant Spanghorn, you'll take up Captain Winters' duties.'

Spranghorn, a big, silent, dark-haired young officer, saluted.

The general nodded dismissal to Pryor and Reynolds.

'I'll need you with me, Mr. Reynolds,' Custer said.

CHAPTER VIII

Calamity's Decision

Headed for food and sleep, the scouts saluted and left. In the late afternoon they awoke. Sitting Bull and his Sioux arrived at the Fort, and the ferocious, thick-set medicine man was received by General Custer.

Sitting Bull and a couple of sub-chiefs stalked, with impressive dignity, in full paint and beaded leather, with fur tippets and stained eagle feathers, to the porch where Custer awaited them.

The Kid and Reynolds slouched nearby, listening. From a nearby window Libby Custer peeked through the lace curtains.

'How, Pahuska!' Sitting Bull said solemnly.

General Custer bowed slightly.

'How, Sitting Bull!'

Ceremonies proceeded. The Kid looked around for Spotted Fawn, the Sioux renegade with whom he had had the brush, but Spotted Fawn was not in evidence. Apparently Sitting Bull had proceeded with his promised punishment.

Sitting Bull loved to talk, and he began a long speech, mostly complaints, to Custer, who listened with set, grave mien.

'Yellow Hair,' Sitting Bull said, 'my people are starving! The *wasichus* have killed our buffalo and cut our hunting grounds in two with their iron-horse steel. Now they invade the sacred Hills of my forefathers. What does the *wasichu* want? Why does he not put wheels on the Sioux so they can be moved more easily? Always we are pushed back on nothing.'

Custer knew that the Sioux had just complaints against the white men. He had sought to feed the Indians from army stores but red tape and the machinations of Indian agents had blocked him. He had made a trip to Washington, to consult President Ulysses Grant and beg aid for the Indians, only to be rebuffed. And yet he was a soldier, subject to military discipline, forced to obey orders given him.

The commander did his best to soothe Sitting Bull. Food and trinkets were offered the Indians.

Dark fell over the far-off Fort Abraham Lincoln, over the colorful Frontier post. And the Rio Kid, aware that he must start on a hard and fast march back to Cherryville at dawn, leading Captain Winters' force, left the celebration to rest some more.

The muddy river flowed heavy with spring flood between it's wide, flat banks, hedged by screens of cottonwood scrub. Late in the night two men met in this brush cover, two of different races. The red man slid silently up, with animal grace, grunting a greeting to the white man awaiting him.

'O, Great Chief, you had my message from Rain-in-the-Face?'

The white man nodded.

'Yeah, Spotted Fawn, I got it, and I wanted to see yuh. But first, what have yuh to say?'

Spotted Fawn had been brought up at an Indian agent's and could speak excellent English.

'Our friend Murphy, the man with canoe belly legs,' he began, 'told me to ride swiftly to tell you of great trouble made by two army scouts, one known as the Rio Kid, who moves like the lightning flash; and Reynolds, the Hunter-Who-Never-Goes-Out-For-Nothing. These caused us heavy losses, attacking us in the dark as we were about to slay a large party of *wasichus* in the Hills. Most of our mustangs were stampeded by the cunning of this Rio

Kid, whose scalp I shall wear at my belt one day.'

The White Chief cursed hotly.

'Damn his heart and soul! I'll nail his hide to the fence, Spotted Fawn!'

'This'—Spotted Fawn took a bowie-knife from his belt—'belongs to the Rio Kid, Great Chief. It fell from its sheath when he attacked me. Rain-in-the-Face hid it under his blanket and later gave it to me.'

'Lemme have it. May come in handy . . . Here's a letter yuh must run to Kansas Joe fast as yuh kin, savvy? Custer's sendin' a troop of cavalry, guided by this same Rio Kid pole-cat, to burn Cherryville. They start at dawn. Murphy's to ambush that advance guard and wipe 'em out, disguised as Sioux.'

'That is war!' cried Spotted Fawn, his dark eyes glowing red.

'Yes, it's war! Murphy won't be able to hold Cherryville when Custer hits. We must be ready to take what we want in the Hills when the time comes and I'll have that Deadwood Gulch! It's worth millions. Make certain Murphy's boys are well got-up as Indians this time. Tell the fools to use unshod mustangs and keep their mouths shut, and to leave no sign to show that whites done the job on that advance guard. After he's attacked 'em he's to hide out in the Black Hills, at the Box Canyon . . . How about that big bunch of settlers that escaped?'

Spotted Fawn shrugged. 'When horses had finally been roped, Great Chief, I heard Murphy order three who are good trailers to pursue them, locate them if they could.'

'Huh! Yuh'd better make shore of 'em, and see they're finished off, Spotted Fawn. That, and the attack on the troops'll force the U.S. to open the Hills. Then I'll make my grab.'

'Ssh!' warned Spotted Fawn suddenly. 'Someone comes!'

It was too late. They had been engrossed in their talk, and a man, walking unsteadily, his footsteps in the soft dirt drowned by the rushing of the river near at hand, came upon them.

'Hey, who the hell's that?' he said, seeing the dark figures before him.

His army blue showed that he was a soldier coming back from leave in town. He had ferried across the river and landed on the bank below the usual dock, when his craft had been swept by the strong current.

He peered intently at the elaborately garbed Indian, and at the Great Chief, coming closer. Suddenly he stopped, came to attention, saluted.

'Sorry, suh—sorry. I didn't know 'twas—'

At that instant Spotted Fawn flicked out his red arm, snakelike. The knife drove deep in under the heart. The half-drunken soldier sank at their feet with a feeble grunt.

'Huh!' growled the Chief. 'Leave the knife

71

and let's get outa here, Spotted Fawn. Ride, now, pronto.'

'I go, Great Chief.'

'*Adios* and hurry.'

With a spat curse the Great Chief tossed his glowing cigar end into the swift muddy water and turned off, while Spotted Fawn, with written orders to Kansas Joe Murphy tucked in a doeskin belt pouch, leaped on his wild, blanket-backed mustang and drove in the cruel spurs tied to his bare ankles.

A fiendish ambush was planned for the Rio Kid and the cavalry he was to lead on Cherryville, death that would strike without warning . . .

Billy North awoke, feeling weak but clear-headed. The sun was creeping up into an azure sky, and the scent of wild flowers was in the June air.

A woman squatted beside him, a woman with dark-brown hair showing under a man's beaver hat that was trimmed with a red feather. Her large brown eyes were upon Billy North's bronzed face, and when he looked at her calmly, she grinned.

'So yuh're back with us at last, Billy,' she asked.

'Yeah—reckon so. Who—who are you, Ma'am?'

'Name's Martha Jane Canary, but they call me Calamity Jane.'

'Oh, shore. I should've known. I've heard

tell of yuh. Say where am I? Where's the Kid and Reynolds? And Celestino?'

'The Mex is out huntin' meat for us,' replied Calamity Jane. 'As for yoreself, the Kid and Lonesome Charlie fetched yuh here, outa the Black Hills. Yuh had a nasty head wound, Billy. I've tended yuh best I could.'

Gingerly Billy North raised a hand to the bandage on his head. Calamity Jane had cut off the hair around the wound. 'I feel all right now. Sorta weak, that's all.'

'We'll soon fix that,' Calamity Jane said cheerfully. 'Yuh need buffalo broth and liver, Billy.'

North suddenly started, bit his lip, sitting up.

'Calamity!' he cried. 'What happened to her—to them?'

'What happened to who?' Martha Jane asked.

'Edith. Oh —I mean them folks, Burton's people! A whole army of hombres attacked 'em. We tried to get in and stop it. That's when I got hurt—'

'Take it easy, Billy! Yuh'll stir yoreself up again. Lie down and rest. They got away. I'm shore of it.'

'How so?'

'Well, the Kid and Reynolds seemed to figger so, anyways. Here comes Celestino. He'll tell yuh.'

The slim Mexican youth, left behind by Bob

73

Pryor to take care of Calamity Jane and North, came slipping silently through the woods. He was carrying a joint of deer meat on his shoulder, rifle in hand. He wore moccasins, and had left his high-peaked sombrero in camp, as such interfered with a hunter's progress in creeping through the bush in search of game.

His white teeth flashed a smile to North, who fixed the lean, dark-skinned face with anxious questioning in his eyes.

'Hey, Celestino! What happened to them pilgrims? Jake Burton's party that we tried to save from ambush?'

Mireles threw down the haunch of venison and squatted by North.

'We geeve zem chance to escape, Beely,' he said, shrugging. 'Zat was bes' we could do, outnumbaire' forty to one aftaire you were heet. We stampede zeir mustangs and warn Burton. Eef he deedn't run for eet, he ees mucho fool.'

'Huh!' grunted North, shaking his head.

Vividly he pictured the trim, vivacious Edith Burton whom he had met at Cherryville. As though she were here smiling at him he could see her merry, dark eyes, her cool-looking blue gingham dress and the curly black hair so neatly banded.

'I got to find out,' he muttered. 'If the Sioux or Kansas Joe's hombres got her—'

It was all he could think about. They told

74

him that two days and nights had passed since he had been wounded. Agonizedly the thought that perhaps Edith Burton and her friends were even now taken by cruel foes, in the Black Hills, occupied him.

'I got to ride, folks,' he declared at last. 'I got to foller them into the Hills and see what's happened. I'd as soon die as not.'

Martha Jane shrewdly watched the young hunter's bronzed face, peaked after what he had just gone through. She made no attempt to argue with Billy North, knowing that a girl was concerned.

'She must be mighty purty,' she said softly.

'She is,' replied North.

'But, Beely,' Mireles said, 'ze General, ze Rio Keed, say to wait here for heem. I cannot leave.'

'I ain't askin' yuh to, Celestino. But I'm ridin'. My hoss—did yuh pick him up?'

Mireles shook his black-haired head.

'No. But ees mustang for you, Beely, that ze Keed roped.'

North struggled to his feet. He felt light-headed and his knees were weak, but after awhile strength began to return. Calamity Jane brought him some food, and warm drink, and when he had eaten he knew he could ride.

'I'm all right, and I'm mighty obliged, folks,' North told his two friends. 'I'll need a saddle and a rifle.'

'Yuh can borry 'em from me,' said Calamity

Jane. 'Wait'll I get packed up, Billy, and then we'll start.'

'Huh? You wouldn't think of goin' into the Hills, would yuh?'

Calamity Jane smiled. 'Reckon if yore young lady can stand it, Billy, I can,' she drawled. 'If them Burton people done got away, they'll need supplies. That's jest what I got to sell.'

Nothing North could say changed the cool decision of Martha Jane Canary.

CHAPTER IX

Thunder in the Hill

Early in the afternoon Billy North, on the chestnut mare, trailed by Calamity Jane on her dapple-gray and with her laden pack-horses, swung west for the Black Hills. Celestino Mireles would not go, would not leave the spot where he was to meet his pard, the Rio Kid.

North and his strange companion rode, staying hidden as far as possible in dry gulches, or in the fringes of brush along the streams. North headed as directly as he dared for the shallow valley in which the ambush on the Burton train had been attempted.

The two camped for a time after dark, ate

76

and rested, then continued. In the gray of dawn, Billy North, scouting out ahead of Calamity Jane's pack train, rode cautiously up the ridge and looked over the mist-laden wilderness, with the stream beyond.

His heart jumped in dismay, as he saw a blackened object near the bank of the creek where the Burton camp had stood that night. Touching the chestnut with his spurs, he hurried down and saw that it was the remains of a Conestoga wagon, burned to the wheels. Near at hand lay the picked corpse of a man. Odds and ends of worthless junk were about, empty cans, a broken bottle, a couple of Indian arrows, a pan with a bullet hole in it.

But as he swiftly reconnoitered, he began to take heart. He found only the single dead man, no doubt killed in the fighting that terrible night. Tracks of other wagons, and horses, human beings, showed in the soft bank of the creek, disappearing into the water. He shoved his mare through the shallow, purling stream and on the other side picked up the trail.

The wilderness was silent save for the chirp of early birds and other natural sounds. North saw no danger signals, as he stuck on the Burton tracks. For a time the tracks were easy to follow, as evidently the immigrants had fled pell-mell from the ambush. Then they slowed down. The Kid's trick of stampeding the enemy horses had given them the chance they needed to escape.

He began to breathe more freely as he read this. Other tracks, super-imposed on those of the Burton party, told him that there had been pursuit, but that it had been greatly delayed.

'Mebbe they got away,' he muttered, wiping sweat from his face.

Martha Canary was coming after him slowly, with her packs. She was at home in the wilderness which she faced with the courage and strength of a man.

As the sun came up yellow and warm, casting its rays over the valleys carpeted with colorful wild flowers, over the mighty shadowed peaks of the Black Hills, North came on two more of the Burton wagons. These also had been set afire. But he did not find any signs of a fight which there would have been had the foe caught up with them.

Cutting through a narrow gap where the bush had recently been broken, he rode out onto hardpan, packed so well that it did not take tracks. Rocks strewed this expanse. After running back and forth for a time, he located a few signs, and guessed that the men who sought to pursue Burton had also been puzzled by the disappearance of the tracks.

It was not long until he found some return tracks of the pursuers, but nothing to show that they had overtaken their prey.

With relief he hunted for further sign of the Burton party, but it was now difficult to pick up. He lost the trail again and again.

At darkness the hunter and Calamity Jane camped. Next day they pushed on into the rising Black Hills. Rugged, gigantic mountains rose all about them, and in the south distance was Harney's Peak, highest point east of the Rockies. Black spruce covered the slopes, and gorgeous rock buttes stuck up toward the summer sky. This was a wilderness paradise, hardly touched by man. Forbidden ground, the home of the gods of the Dakotas.

Halfway through the following day's ride, Billy North proceeded by guess, only now and then able to check that he was on the right track by some slight hint. Then a thin column of blue smoke caught his alert eyes.

He swung and rode back to warn Calamity Jane, who concealed herself and her mounts in some timber, while North rode forward to investigate.

Later, to the South, the hunter lay flat on a high butte, peering out across a great sweep of mountain country, cut by shadowed deep canyons. In the distance his keen eyes sighted a column of Indians, hundreds on hundreds of them, slowly coming in from the southwest to the Hills.

'The Sioux!' he muttered.

They had their squaws with them, each travois laden with hide tepee and belongings. The fierce red warriors, some with buffalo horns sticking from temples, others wearing full feather head-dress and clad in beaded buckskin, rode their wild little mustangs through the Hills of their forefathers.

North watched the great array of redskins slowly proceeding, saw them stop and go into camp on a level stretch along a river bank. The smoke column he had seen had come from a scout's fire, signaling the main band on.

He slid back of the butte, returning to Calamity.

'We can't ride durin' the day any more,' he said. 'The Sioux are in.'

They concealed themselves, and once during the afternoon heard the voices of Sioux hunters not far from them, but were not discovered. The Indians were mounted on shaggy ponies and did not come far enough up to cut what slight sign they had left.

Before the sun set, one of the sudden, terrific thunderstorms that so terrorized the Sioux in the Hills came up. The whole world grew black as night, with weird, long flashes of lightning intermittently illuminating the sky, while thunder shook the mountains.

'Better get things tied down and hold the hosses,' North told Calamity, and they made ready for the onslaught of the elements.

The rain began, big drops spattering on the leaves and grass. Then the heavens seemed to open and water poured so heavily on them they might as well have been in a flowing stream. Wet to the hide in no time at all, unable to see, they were beaten by the rain. Hail fell, too, stinging like pebbles.

The storm did not last long, but its violence was stunning. As the sky reddened over the Black Hills in its last appearance of the day, Calamity and North, soaked and bewildered, took stock of themselves and their possessions.

They were still wet when night fell. Billy and his comrade swung a wide circle northward of the valley where stood the main Sioux village. Under the stars and a slice of moon they traveled on west. Strange-shaped buttes looked like threatening monsters, the granite abutments dwarfing trees, making men look like ants. Needle spires thrust up, hard cores left after erosion of softer strata.

They were far into the Hills, in that eerie land where certain parts of the mountains were never entered by Indians, being reserved for the Great Spirit and His medicine men.

The hard rain had flattened out grass and earth, and covered the few marks left by Burton's party. North had lost it, and was unable to pick it up again.

'Must be somewheres round here, Calamity,' he said to the woman. 'They'll keep quiet, jest like us.'

Hidden in a woods that day, they slept. But, after a time, something brought Billy North awake and he came up on his knees, gun in hand.

As soon as Billy moved, Calamity Jane opened her eyes and gripped her rifle, which was always at her side.

'What is it, Billy?' she whispered.

'I hear voices,' he replied, in the same low tone.

He crept through the brush-choked woods in which they had been hiding, and at the outer skirt looked down a long, slanting hill. Beyond that were great rocks, heavily bushed, choked by trees and shale thrown into a mad confusion. It seemed impassable, on the west black pines rose in steps to a high crest. North observed that many of the trees had been burned.

Then he saw a man emerge from what looked like the flat surface of a huge granite cliff, and he started at sight of this apparition. A moment later he recognized Jed Sloan, the blond-haired giant, one of Burton's followers.

Sloan had a rifle in one hand, the ever-present Sharps, and was no doubt going on a hunt. Right behind Sloan appeared Jake Burton. The bluff, heavy leader of the immigrants stopped and watched Sloan start up the slope.

North was about to hail them when his keen ear caught a rustle in front of him, and he crouched, frozen where he was, hunting for the source of the noise. It took his trained vision several moments to pick out the buckskin-clad Indians lying in a nest of grayish rocks, fringed by brush. They were not over a hundred yards in front of him, toward Burton and Sloan.

He glimpsed a stirring eagle feather, the glint of light on a leveled rifle barrel. Calamity Jane, who was up beside North by now, squatted close at his left.

'I'll take the one on this side, Billy,' she breathed.

But as the two threw their guns to shooting position, cocking their weapons, one of the Indians fired, an instant-fraction ahead of them.

Jed Sloan was whipped around as by a giant hand, and he fell, rolling down the slope. Calamity Jane's rifle snapped at North's ear as he let go a fast one. The second Indian, whose gun muzzle had been on Jake Burton, never pulled trigger. He took lead that finished him where he lay. And Calamity's slug had taken care of the man who had plugged Sloan.

Leaping up, North sang out to Burton, who had jumped toward the fallen Sloan, drawing a pistol from his belt.

'Look out, Billy!' cried Calamity. 'There's another one up on the hill!'

From the corner of his eye, North saw a mounted Sioux jerking the reins of the mustang he rode. Two other mounts stood nearby, the horses of the pair who had been shot.

A bullet whizzed within an inch of North's head. He threw his rifle to his shoulder and tried to get the third man. Bent low over his animal the Indian galloped full-tilt back out of sight across the crest of the hill, and North saw leaves shiver as his own slug zipped through them.

Billy North went and stooped over the two Indians. They were dead. He cursed with amazement as he examined them. 'What is it, Billy?' asked Calamity, coming up.

'Ain't Sioux. They're whites, fixed up like Indians, Calamity! I know one of 'em. He's from Cherryville, Kansas Joe's camp.'

North arose and went to meet Jake Burton, while Calamity Jane returned to bring up her pack-horses.

Burton looked up, sadly shaking his head as Billy North, rifle in the crook of his arm, came up.

'Sloan's dead,' the burly leader said. 'Reckon I'd be, if it hadn't been for you, North. Never knew them Sioux were up there.'

'They ain't Sioux,' North said promptly. 'They're whites fixed up like 'em. One got away, which is bad news for us, Burton. There's over a thousand Sioux a day's run from here . . . Where's yore camp?'

'Hid in that deadwood gulch,' growled Burton.

He was shaken by Sloan's sudden death. He stood up, his jaw set. But like others in that tough era, he realized that death struck often and swiftly on the Frontier.

Calamity Jane ambled up, fetching the horses.

'Who's he?' asked Burton.

'It's a her,' replied North, as Calamity grinned. 'Calamity Jane, they call her. She's a mighty good scout. She's got some stuff mebbe yuh'll wish to buy.'

Martha Jane blinked at the dead Sloan.

'It's a dirty shame,' she muttered, as she saw he was gone. 'The devils!'

'I shore hate to tell his woman,' groaned Burton.

'Well, c'mon. We'll have to bury these dead ones. Dunno how long we'll have 'fore that feller who got away fetches back his pards. Where's yore camp, Burton?'

CHAPTER X

The Stockade

North headed for the deadwood gulch, with its burned stretches of pines as Burton led the way. The entrance was hidden by the big rocks and bush. Only by going right up close to it could the passage be found, a narrow way just wide enough to lead a horse through.

'We hid our wagons, and toted what we

could on packs,' explained Burton. 'Had a mighty narrow escape, two nights out from Cherryville.'

'I know,' growled North. 'I was there.'

'Shore he was,' chimed in Calamity. 'Pore feller near got kilt savin' yuh, Burton.'

'Then that was you up on the ridge?' cried Jake.

'Well, I was one of 'em,' replied North modestly. 'Wasn't much account. Got clipped right off. Yuh can thank the Rio Kid and Charlie Reynolds. The Kid stampeded the enemy hosses and give yuh a chance to escape.'

'We didn't quit runnin' for seventy hours,' declared Burton. 'Lost one man in the battle and several got pinked. Whenever wagons busted down we deserted 'em.'

They came out into a tortuously twisting, narrow and deep gulch, with a creek running along the bottom. Making a turn, North could see men knee-deep in the stream, washing sand in flat pans; placer mining. Under a beetling cliff stood the camp where women were busy at various tasks—breadmaking, drying venison, washing.

Billy North's heart leaped with happiness as he saw Edith Burton rise up from a tub of clothes and stare at him.

'Howdy, ma'am,' he cried.

Danger and sadness were banished at sight of her, and he felt he was in the right place, the place destined for him. The restlessness which had been upon him ever since he had first met this girl was soothed, and in its place came a deep content.

She took his outstretched hand, smiling up at him.

'How'd you get here?' she asked.

'I hope yuh ain't sorry to see me!'

Color touched her cheeks. 'I'm not sorry. I'm glad.'

Jake Burton was trying to tell Mrs. Sloan of her young mate's fate, but the woman had already read it in his eyes. The shooting had been heard and though they believed it was the hunters firing at animals, the pall of Indian attack was always over them.

Edith heard the terrible tidings and grew sober.

'I'll have to try to comfort her, Mr. North,' she whispered. She touched his hand and went to the young widow who sat staring out blindly across the gulch.

Burton wiped cold sweat from his gray-haired brow. Billy North stepped to his side as Calamity Jane mingled with the women.

'Looka here, Burton, yuh're in a dangerous position, down in this gulch,' North said. 'Yuh're hid, but if yuh're smelled out they'll have yuh. One of Murphy's men got away jest now, and from what I savvy of them skunks, if they don't come back themselves with a big gang, they'll sic the Sioux on yuh. From the other side there, yuh could be picked off at will.'

'Right enough,' agreed Jake Burton. 'We been so busy pickin' up gold we jest stayed put.'

'So yuh've found gold!'

'To the grass roots! Millions here, Billy. Richest claims I ever see.'

'Yuh can't file claims here, though. This is Sioux land, forbidden to white men.'

Burton's face darkened, hardened. The madness of gold's lure had entered his soul as it did the hearts of all prospectors. Nothing could check such a fever or the determination which sent hardy pioneers westward, crushing all opposition before them. Always there was this struggle between red and white civilizations.

'We ain't givin' this up, Sioux or no Sioux,' growled Burton, with a chip on his shoulder. 'I'm glad yuh're here, Billy, if yuh wish to stay with us, but we didn't ask yuh to come. We can take care of ourselves.'

'It don't look like it,' snapped Billy North. 'Get a couple of men out there with shovels and bury them dead ones, savvy? I'll cover the sign myself. The Hills are swarmin' with Sioux, to say nothin' of white men who'd murder every one of yuh for a gold strike like yuh say yuh got here. I'm stickin' with yuh. I don't want any Sioux gold, but I aim to guard yuh. Yuh'll have to build a real stockade and set a regular watch.'

Burton stared, frowning, into the hunter's steely eyes. Then he shrugged.

'All right, Billy, have it yore own way. Reckon I'm mighty glad yuh've come.'

In Billy's North's veins ran the blood of adventurers, and he was sticking to his own kind through thick and thin. It was a matter of viewpoint—the whites struggling with the reds for control of a vast continent.

North got on well with most Indians, and liked many of them. But a pretty young girl's magnetic charm, the mightiest of magic, drew him, and nothing could turn him.

Alone of them all, North, brought up on the Frontier, realized fully what constant and terrible peril they were in, with the Sioux swarming in the Hills. Every precaution must be taken against massacre of their fighting men, capture and enslavement of young women and children.

There was also the fact that one of Kansas Joe Murphy's disguised gunnies had got away. North believed it only a matter of time before their enemies would return and strike.

By evening of the next day, North, using every hand in camp though they hated to quit hunting gold, had up a stockade of thick pine poles, sharpened at both ends, and driven in the ground, laced together by long withes of cedar roots as tough as rawhide. The horses were hidden in a natural corral some distance from camp so as not give them away.

Ammunition and supplies were placed under canvas and brush shelters inside the stockade, concealed in protecting rocks on a high point up from the gulch across the creek.

Then, with everything as set as he could make it, North let the placer miners go back to work in the winding creek. But he went to stand guard on a high butte to the east from which he could sweep the surrounding country for miles, his watchful eyes protecting the girl he adored.

'They won't get us for nothin',' he mused.

Often, in the succeeding days, he caught signs of the Sioux, a puff of distant smoke, or birds flying from the path of red hunters. Twice he sighted groups of savages, but they did not approach the deadwood gulch.

'Reckon that spy went back to report to Murphy,' he thought. 'They shore ain't tipped off the Sioux yet!'

But he was sure that soon would come a moment when Burton's folks would bless the stockade that North had forced them to build. The Sioux were close to open war, a war precipitated by the evil machination of a white man, and yet inevitable in the struggle between the two races.

'Wonder what the Kid and Reynolds are up to?' muttered North.

He could not guess. Dark was closing in, so he took his rifle and slid back toward camp . . .

The Rio Kid had his Ree Indian scouts spread out in a fan formation a mile in advance of the thin column of U. S. cavalry as it wound through the rough wilderness toward Cherryville, Kansas Joe Murphy's thieving, murderous camp.

There were no wagons with this flying column. Pack-horses carried all necessary supplies of food and ammunition. They were to hurry under Custer's orders, given to Captain Frank Winter, to Cherryville, there to destroy the camp and capture as many prisoners as possible.

Lieutenants, non-coms rode in position on the flanks—seasoned troopers and Indian fighters, broken-in and trained by Custer. Gear was orderly. They carried Spencer carbines, revolvers and pouches of ammunition, with rolled packs at saddle cantles. Leather creaked and thudding hoofs beat dust into the warm air of the Dakota summer.

The valley picked by the Kid formed a natural route south. It was narrowing to great bluffs, granite giants between which the troops must pass to reach the creek headwaters on which Cherryville stood.

Pryor's keen, slitted blue eyes sought the silent, brooding heights. They ran for a quarter of a mile, too constricted for his liking, to be the exit from the long valley they were in. Pine woods, blackly dense, came to the edge of the granite, topped by fringe of bush.

Pryor had no reason to expect trouble up here, but a good scout was always alert and ready, never took chances.

'Long Back!' he called.

Long Back, a lean, dark-skinned Red Indian, in a pair of cavalry trooper's discarded pants with the wide yellow stripe faded and half gone, and naked torso, came trotting his bare-backed, hairy horse to the Kid. He nudged the mustang on with his bare, splay feet.

Long Back was the Kid's Indian lieutenant of scouts, a trusted man. There was implacable enmity between the Rees and Sioux, the latter having decimated Long Back's tribe until there were but a small number of them left.

A rattlesnake skin band was tight about Long Back's black-haired head. His cheekbones were sharply high in his lean, leathery face, as fierce as a tiger's, and in his buckskin belt were knife and gun.

'Dismount yore men and git up on them bluffs,' Pryor ordered the Indian.

'Ugh,' agreed Long Back. 'No smell right, Cap!'

A sergeant with three stripes on his arm

came galloping up from the column, still a quarter of a mile from the scouts.

'Cap'n Winters wants yuh at once,' the sergeant said, coughing dust from his throat.

'All right, Durham.'

'His hors dropped a shoe,' the sergeant told the lithe Kid. 'Yuh'll find him at the back of the column.'

'Right.' He spoke to Long Back again. 'Go to it, Long Back. Check those bluffs.'

The Ree saluted and, signaling his men, they dismounted and started slowly up the steep slopes. It would take some time to work around to the narrow points.

CHAPTER XI

Ambush

Pryor shoved Saber back toward the troopers. Lieutenant Jack Green, a smooth-faced kid fresh from West Point, and on his first rcal foray, was in charge of the van.

The Kid pulled up for a moment to speak to the young officer.

'Hold till yuh hear from me, Lieutenant,' he said. 'I'll be right back.'

'All right, Kid.'

The order to halt rang out, and then came the at ease order. The troopers waited in their saddles, glad to rest.

Pryor rode on back, passing the thin line of troopers. They all knew him, liked him.

The burly Winters was standing to one side while a trooper blacksmith was hammering a new shoe on the captain's charger. Two men in blue uniform, covered with dust, their horses sweated from a long ride, stood at attention close at hand. They had just arrived, but the Kid recognized them as troopers he had seen among the men at Fort Abraham Lincoln. They had evidently been sent on from the Fort, and had just caught up, after a hard ride to catch the raiding party.

'Yuh want me, Cap'n?' asked the Kid.

To his surprise, Captain Winters turned a scowling face upon him. All through the trip, the Kid had got on well with the troop leader. Frank Winters had seemed much happier in action than he had at the post.

Burly in his blue tunic with its insignia, with his army Stetson curving over his wind-burned face, Winters' brown eyes now were hard. His face was set, and his close-clipped mustache twitched as it was apt to do when the captain was under strain.

'Pryor, yuh're under arrest!' said Winters. 'I have a written order here from General Custer to turn yuh over to these troopers for immediate return to the Fort.'

'What!' cried the astounded Kid. 'The general orders my arrest? Yuh must be loco,

Cap'n!'

Winters reddened, darkening under his heavy tan.

'No doubt of the signature,' he growled. 'It's for murder of a soldier near the Fort. Unbuckle yore guns and put yoreself in charge of these—'

From the south, sudden smashing volleys of heavy guns rang out. Shrill whoops, blood-curdling in their shrieking reverberations, split the valley air. Then the *crack-crack* of carbines and hoarse shouts of men rose in a confused bedlam.

Frank Winters cursed wildly and leaped for his horse, knocking the blacksmith out of his way as he swung into the saddle.

'To hell with the shoe!' he bawled. 'Bugler, blow the charge!'

'No, Cap'n not through the gap!' shouted the Rio Kid.

He guessed what had occurred, cursing the order that had brought him back from the narrow point.

'That fool Green's as headstrong as an unbroke mustang pinin' for some trouble,' he muttered, as Winters, excited by the sudden attack, drove in his spurs and, saber held high, whirled south.

The bugler, always near the commander, was unshipping the instrument. The Rio Kid reached out, snatched the bugle from the trooper's surprised lips and set the dun after

Winters. With the fire so hot from the south end of the valley he knew that hundreds of rifles were in action.

'What the hell!' he thought angrily. 'Green musta got impatient and started through that gap, the fool!'

'Hey, you! Halt! Yuh're under arrest!'

'That'll have to wait, Trooper,' the Kid bawled back, as the dun flew after Winters.

Saber snorted with pleasure as he raced to the fight. He loved the smell of powder, the crash of battle.

A carbine bullet whizzed over the Kid's lowered head, a slug sent by one of the troopers who had been ordered to arrest him, but he paid no attention. Full tilt, he drove on, and could see the welter of fallen troopers and horses blocking the path between the granite bluffs.

Heavy guns boomed from both sides of the high pass, up above, pouring death into the massed troopers. Eagle feathers, painted faces, could be glimpsed as men popped up to shoot.

As the Kid rode he kept working up the side. He threw the bugle to his lips and blew, not the charge, but retreat.

The thin notes of the bugle slowed the troopers. But Frank Winters, stunned by the surprise of the ambush, was urging his squadron leaders on.

The Rio Kid rode as far as he could up the

precipitous slope. The shooting kept on, hot and heavy. Pryor flung himself from his horse when Saber could no longer advance, and ran on. Long Back was coming from the pine forest, running full speed, leaping from point to point with the agility of a mountain goat.

'No come—no come!' he shouted to the Kid. 'Troopers stay back. Bush full with Sioux, Cap!'

Bob Pryor, cursing, glimpsed the death in the pass—death of the advance guard which had been led by young Green. A dozen soldiers were down, and horses kicked and milled about them.

The Rio Kid dashed on, and after a moment Long Back came after him.

Both Colts in hand, the Kid made the pine woods over the western bluff. There he could look down, see the Indians in the granite rocks, crouched behind screens of brush.

He began to shoot madly, but with a cool aim that made every bullet count. Feeling his responsibility for the safety of the column, the Kid took his revenge with icy fury.

Long Back and one of his Rees came creeping up beside Pryor and opened fire on the rear of the attackers.

Down below in the valley, Captain Frank Winters, his saber flashing in the sun, was urging his fighting men on. The bugles were beginning to sound the charge.

'Get into 'em, Long Back!' snapped the Kid.

With the thrill of battle heating his blood, he jumped up from his rock shelter, scuttled forward, both guns smashing bullets into the barbaric figures he could glimpse on the bluffs. Long Back and his Ree companion were shooting remorselessly.

The Kid cast himself down behind a rise, reloading rapidly. He bobbed up again to pour lead into the enemy who were as thick as leaves in the bush.

Long Back's friend threw up both hands, without a sound, and pitched over dead. Bullets whistled about the lithe Kid, crouched behind rock shelter. They bit off chunks of stone, spattering some into his eyes. Then he was up, his Colts blasting the line of foes.

Across the narrow gap were more feathered, painted men, seeking to destroy the troops below. The Spencers were aimed up at them, but the angle was not satisfactory. They could not reach the enemy, while the attackers above could rise up and let go as they pleased.

For minutes it seemed that Winters would cram his men into the constricted gap in the confusion of the skirmish, and there they would be easy prey for the ambushers. But the Kid's hard, insistent fire, abetted by Long Back's carbine, was taking its toll.

Shrieks of rage arose in the throats of those he sought to break. More and more guns swung to answer the Rio Kid's Colts.

Some of the ambushers were using .50-

caliber Sharps, the great guns *whooshing* with the sound of exploding cannon as the heavy slugs split the air.

A bullet drove a wide hole in the Kid's hat. He felt the slug's ominous death kiss in his curly chestnut hair. Something bit a chunk of flesh from his left forearm, but he kept shooting, hotly, determinedly.

The ambushers could not stand this hot fire in their backs. A bunch jumped up and ran along the bluff, heading for a screen of pines. Long Back and the Kid knocked two of them sprawling, then swung their guns on the other side, dropping bullets over there.

The mad confusion and bedlam of the battle clashed on the warm afternoon air. The wilderness rang with the sounds of struggling, blood-maddened fighters.

These seconds seemed like hours, as the Kid, with only Long Back to help him, strove to break up the ambush.

Impelled by panic, more and more of the figures in Indian garb were deserting the bluffs. From below, the disciplined firing of seasoned troops, who knew how to die fighting, against any odds, sought for the foe.

But it was the Rio Kid who checked the massacre, kept down the death toll among the cavalrymen. Unceasing, lips grim, powder blackening his handsome, reckless face, Bob Pryor smashed a hundred or more of the killers.

The attackers dared not run toward him in the face of such deadly, accurate fire as the Kid and the Ree tossed into them.

'Keep it up!' bawled the Kid. 'They're losin' their nerve!'

His eardrums were roaring from the explosions. It seemed as though the world were one vast banging.

Bugle tones pierced the bedlam, the clear, long-drawn-out notes sounding the dismount order.

'At last!' muttered the Kid, wiping sweaty dirt from his eyes, so that he might take better aim.

The troopers, throwing themselves from their horses, carbines in hand, were starting up the sides of the valley, to get around in back of the ambushers.

'About time,' thought the Kid.

He jumped to his feet to follow the mass of men south toward the woods. The ambushers were in full retreat now, aware that their ambush had only been partially successful, thanks to Pryor's swift work.

Afoot, speeding them with his Colts that were hot in his calloused hands, the Rio Kid pursued the foe, reckless of their answering bullets.

A dozen of the attackers who had paid with their lives for their attack on the troopers lay along the granite bluff. A second bunch, on the other side of the gap, seeing their pards on the run, took to their heels, dropping out of sight as they scuttled away south.

'Horses down there,' grunted Long Back, as he and the Rio Kid paused to shove fresh shells into their hot and smoky guns.

Through the black trunks of the pines, the Kid saw the Indian figures leaping to the backs of mustangs. They rode rapidly off, out of his sight, strung out in a ragged line.

'Forty of 'em on this side, more on the other,' he figured.

A parting volley, and the Kid stopped at the edge of the woods. They were on their way, and he could not chase them afoot.

CHAPTER XII

Arrest

Gasping for wind from the hard run, and from the terrific battle, the Rio Kid swung and worked down to the bodies on the bluff.

Shooting had begun to die off, as the enemy retreated on fast mustangs. The cavalry bugles sounded the charge, and Captain Winters led a squadron forward, picking a way through the dead in the pass.

But the army plugs were no match for the plains mustangs, and the barbaric devils were gone in a few swift dashes, out of sight and gunshot into the wilderness.

The Kid bent over a corpse, examining the Sioux form. In beaded buckskin suit, moccasins, skin hat with feather, and face heavily painted with daubs of red, yellow and blue, at first glance the dead man would have been thought to be an Indian. But the Kid and Long Back knew better.

'Wasichu!' grunted Long Back, as he drew his scalping knife. He was disappointed. He would have preferred a Sioux scalp.

'Yeah, a white man, one of Kansas Joe Murphy's gang,' said the Kid. 'This is the second time I've found a Murphy man in Indian disguise.'

The Kid arose, shrugged, and then worked his way down into the valley. A whistle brought the dun dancing up to him. Saber had been in the thick of the fray, enjoying himself in the crash of battle.

Dazed soldiers were staring at their dead. In the pass lay young Green, the lieutenant who had impetuously led his men into the gap against the Kid's advice. About ten dead troopers lay around him, and a number of horses. More troopers had wounds. But the bulk of them had been saved by Pryor.

'Hey, you!'

Pryer swung in his saddle, to see the two troopers from the Fort.

'Yuh're under arrest,' one of them growled.

'All right.'

102

The Kid shrugged and rolled a cigarette, waiting for the return of Captain Frank Winters.

'Winters has got nerve, but he could use more brains,' he mused.

It was half an hour before the captain came riding back at the head of his squadron. They had been easily evaded by the fast Indian mustangs.

Winters' face was covered with blood and dirt. He had lost his Stetson, and his thick, sandy hair was matted with sweat. His tunic was unbuttoned at the throat, showing his bull neck. The officer's brown eyes, narrowed in the glare of the sunlight, took in his dead and wounded. The odor of blood was nauseating.

He snapped some orders to his subordinates about cleaning up, and the bugles blew. Slouched in his leather, head bowed, he rode back along the line, and the Rio Kid faced him.

'A close shave, Winters,' the Rio Kid said, pushing his dun close so that only the captain heard. 'Lieutenant Green lost his head. And that gap was no place to charge men through!'

Pryor was not under military discipline as a civilian scout. Captain Frank Winters had just been saved from a serious disaster by the Kid's swift work. Winters knew he had made a mistake, and was still angry and shaken.

The burly captain glared into the Kid's blue eyes.

'There's yore prisoner,' he snapped to the pair of troopers from the Fort. 'Take him!'

'Better lemme stick with yuh till yuh're through at Cherryville, Cap'n,' the Rio Kid drawled.

'Take him!' roared Winters, turning his horse, his broad back hunched as he rode off.

The Kid passed over his gun belts and Colts, but said nothing about the hidden weapons in shoulder holsters under his clothing. With a trooper on either side of him, he trotted the dun up the valley, away from the soldiers who were going into bivouac, to bury their dead and treat the wounded.

The sun was lowering in the sky when they had ridden a couple of miles up the wide valley where dips and trees hid them from the troops. The two soldiers guarding the Kid talked as they rode, mostly about Bismarck town and the pleasures it offered.

'Boys,' the Kid drawled suddenly, 'who the hell give yuh the orders to come after the column and arrest me?'

'Huh?' said the taller of the two. 'Why, Lieutenant Spanghorn done sent us. Said the general wished it.'

'Was there a killin' up there?'

'Yeah. Trooper Wells of Troop C got stabbed in the back, near the river. It was yore knife they found, feller, stuck in him.'

'I thought so, wonderin' what this was all about. Then I remembered that I had lost my knife, back in the bush somewheres. Reckon somebody picked it up. Who said it was my knife?'

'Shucks, I dunno. Mebbe 'twas Charlie Reynolds, come to think of it.'

'Somebody,' the Kid mused to himself, 'wanted to get rid of me. That ambush proves they was all set and waitin' for us down here. Long Back's a smart scout, but he needs guidin'. Hope Winters takes to heart the lesson he learnt today.'

But he was worried. The long arm of his hidden foe was reaching for him. There was suspicion in his mind. Of course Custer might have been convinced somehow that he had murdered a soldier in a row, and perhaps the arrest was bona-fide. But he was not at all certain of that.

For a time he carefully watched the two troopers, Riley and Keene, for any attempt to shoot him as he rode, but they were plainly simple soldiers carrying out orders. And they meant to take him back, for they rode just at his elbows, slightly behind, so that he could not make any sudden dash into the woods off the trail.

The Kid was pulling himself together. The weariness after the hard skirmish at twin bluffs was passing. His wounds, gashes and scratches which were of no serious consequence were roughly bound, and under him stepped the fastest horse on the Frontier, the dun with the black stripe down his back.

Saber picked up his hoofs high as he moved. In the Civil War he had been Captain Robert Pryor's mount and loved to lead a company. While he objected as a rule to the proximity of other horses, when the riders were in uniform he would control his temper. Of a bullying nature with other mustangs, able to forage for himself and enjoying a fight in his equine way as much as his master did in his, Saber considered himself quite a privileged character.

A dry grin touched the Kid's handsome face.

'Yuh needn't strut so, Saber,' he muttered. 'This ain't no dress parade. We're under arrest.'

Still, it was no joke. Custer had entrusted him with the safety of the troopers. And knowing the forces of evil in Cherryville and the might of Kansas Joe's gang, that had hardly been touched by the damage the Kid had inflicted, Pryor was worried.

'I reckon I won't ride all the way back to the Fort,' he decided. 'Hell or high water, I'll carry out orders.'

It was growing late. The setting sun was ruby red over the Black Hills that towered eight thousand feet into the sky, miles westward. As the Kid docilely rode on, Riley and Keene, the arresting troopers, lost some of their alertness.

'Figger it's time to camp for the night, Tim,'

Riley said at last.

'Uh-huh,' grunted Keene. 'Mister, pull up there. We'll lay up in them pines till mornin'.'

The Kid obediently swung Saber off the trail toward the pines. The two troopers dismounted. With a single movement Pryor whirled the dun around to face them as they were busy with their reins, and whipped a six-shooter from inside his blue shirt. Its bulge beneath his powerful arm had been hidden by his open vest.

'Hate to do this to yuh, boys,' he drawled, 'but I don't fancy goin' all the way to Lincoln on a false charge. I got work to do.'

'Why, damn yore hide!' shouted Trooper Riley.

But seeing the round black muzzle of the steady Colt, and the stern set of the Kid's face, he raised his arms. Keene followed suit.

'Step back with yore paws reachin',' ordered Pryor, 'and walk a ways up trail. I'll leave yore hosses, but if yuh try to take me it means tall trouble.'

Under his gun the troopers obeyed. Hands elevated, they walked to the military road. The Kid picked his gun-belts from Riley's saddle-horn, strapped them on, and on the dun trailed the soldiers a short distance north. He wanted to make sure they did as he commanded, and wished to run them a safe distance from their plugs.

There was a jumble of rocks and thick bush

107

a couple of hundred yards north, a bend in the path. And as the Kid moved, his eyes upon the troopers, a bullet bit a chunk from his ear.

For a shocked instant he believed that somehow one of the troopers had fired on him, but both had their hands up and had paused in amazement at the shriek of the slug.

Whirling the dun, Pryor galloped west into the trees, but looked back over his right shoulder. The soft summer breeze was carrying off a grayish smoke puff that had come from over the thicketed rise north on the trail, widened by the passage of Captain Winters' force. The Kid threw a couple of six-gun bullets up there.

'Somebody tryin' to pick me off with a rifle,' he muttered, pistol gripped hard in his bronzed hand. 'That was a Spencer, too!'

The Spencer carbine was in use by the army.

The two troopers were alarmed by the fire from the hidden ambush. They raced away, to throw themselves flat in cover.

Bob Pryor spurred Saber west, and found a ridgy rise up which he could ride north. Someone was gunning for him, in every possible way, he figured, and he was eager to find who it was.

There was not much more daylight left, so he hustled on, hoping to get up behind the rough ground from which he had seen the smoke puff.

He had to cross an open space to make it. He slowed, his Colt ready for action, his narrowed eyes hunting the dense thickets and needle rocks. Then the sound of clopping hoofs, dimming to the north, came to him, and he knew his foe must be in retreat, unwilling to match guns with the Rio Kid.

Dismounting close to the thickets, he pushed through, Colt up and ready. He had noted the spot from which the powder smoke had risen, and quickly located the pressed grass, broken twigs, and still slowly-moving withes of brush coming back into place.

His enemy had a good start, and within a few minutes night would fall. Stooping, he picked up the discharged cartridge case, a Spencer carbine shell, army ammunition. Then his keen scrutiny caught the glint of gold. It was a button, with U. S. in raised letters on its curved face. Several blue threads and a tiny, irregular patch of cloth were attached to the loop. As the owner of that button had moved, belly to ground as he sought to drygulch the Kid, the button had been torn off by a projecting sharp piece of rock shelf.

'Reckon I made him jump with my bullets,' Bob Pryor muttered.

A shout from the south, and the *zip* of a slug through the branches told him he had forgotten something—the two troopers from whom he had escaped. He had no desire to shoot either of them so, leaping to his feet, he ran to the dun, leaped into the saddle, and cut for the pines.

The soldiers pursued him on their cavalry plugs, and sent wild lead singing after the Rio Kid, riding low over his horse. But the government mounts were not in Saber's class, and as night dropped its velvet blanket over the wilderness, he streaked through the pines, cut over to the south trail, and headed for Cherryville.

'I ain't lettin' Custer down, no matter what,' he muttered, his chinstrap bunching tight his determined jaw. 'That ambush was nasty. They must have savvied we were comin', to have it set the way they did!'

He meant to scout Kansas Joe Murphy's criminal camp and check up, before Captain Frank Winters rode in with his cavalry. The troopers would go into bivouac for the night, resume their march at dawn. But the Kid would seize these night hours for his scouting. He kept the uniform button, slipped it into one of his saddlebags.

The close call at the valley bluffs had roused all his suspicions, all of his powerful instincts as a scout that had been developed during the Civil War and on the Frontier. He sensed that he was against some powerful combination, directed by a cunning brain.

'Was that him, that drygulcher back there?' he wondered.

CHAPTER XIII

Hidden Camp

When the Rio Kid had ridden well around Winters' position it was late and the moon was up. He slid from his leather and patted the dun.

'Quiet, now, Saber!' he murmured, and slipped through the woods toward Cherryville.

He could see the rough buildings in the darkness, but there were no lights on. The big warehouse in which Charlie Reynolds had discovered the stolen army supplies, stood stark and bare. The store and saloon, shacks and tents showed no illumination.

'By gee, they've sashayed—warned shore enough,' he growled.

Winters would ride into a deserted town.

Suddenly he froze, a shadow in shadow, close to the store, at the side away from the moon. A low creaking sound had begun, and the dull thudding of hoofs came to his ears from the warehouse. Flat on his belly he inched forward, seeking to get to a position from which he could command the doors.

'That's the last load, thank hell!' a whiny, high-pitched voice said.

'Soupy Lou Griggs,' thought the Kid.

Bob Pryor would never forget that peculiar

shrill voice of Griggs, one of Murphy's henchmen.

Then a covered wagon, laden high with bales and boxes, swung between the store and the building opposite the Kid. The six horses heaved against the weight, and the driver's bull-whip snapped, crackling on their hides. The wagon hit a downgrade and was driven off westward, quickly dropping from Pryor's sight.

The Kid peeked around the corner of his hiding place and saw several dark figures mounting horses and starting to follow the wagon. He waited, until they were gone, knowing he could trail the vehicle in the light. Anyhow, he wished to check the warehouse.

He made it, easily enough. It was black inside, but he could smell burned oil. They had been using shaded lanterns, and had got all the stolen goods out. The big structure was empty save for odds and ends of scrap, discarded junk strewn on the dirt floor.

Then he whirled, his pistol flying to his hand. Against the lighter rectangle of the doorway he saw the figure of a man coming back in. And there was no other way out except by that single door, no place in which to hide.

The man, obviously unaware that anyone was in there, struck a match, and the yellow flame burned at the stick. He applied the match to a candle stub he held.

He looked up then, and saw the Rio Kid, pistol up, watching him.

'The Kid!'

Curses of terror dribbled from Soupy Lou Griggs' flaccid lips. His weak chin trembled, and he began to shake violently. He had seen this grim avenger in action, and the Colt in Pryor's paw was no comfort. The ratty man, with even his straggly brown mustache quivering, and his close-set eyes rolling, was utterly flabbergasted. Then he began to beg for mercy in his high whine.

'Don't—don't kill me, Kid! Don't! I ain't done nothin', honest. I work for Murphy and —I ain't armed. Hung my gun on that peg over there—come back to get it . . .'

'What the hell are yuh talkin' about, Soupy?' a rough voice demanded, and a whole flock of Murphy's gunnies pushed to the door.

The candle flickered in Soupy Lou's thin hand, and his knees were so flabby he could scarcely stand erect.

Then the others saw the lithe Kid and recognized him. Their arch-enemy was trapped. The Kid, knowing it was shoot his way out or be taken, fired a swift one that ripped the candle from Griggs' paw. Soupy Lou screamed in shrill agony, and as the flame was doused and the stub of candle rolled on the floor, the Kid had a flash of Soupy, with blood spurting from his hand, collapsing where he stood.

'He got me he got me!' shrieked Griggs. 'I'm dyin'! *ow-w!*'

Pryor leaped aside, grabbing a second Colt, flitting forward. A blast of bullets lit the warehouse with blue-yellow eerie glow as the gunnies at the door opened up. The Kid heard the rushing slugs spitting through the air where he had just been standing. Then the *rap-rap-rap* as they tore through the board walls.

In the empty warehouse the explosions were terrific, banging echoes of doom.

Moving like a panther shadow, the Rio Kid ran for the door, holding his fire. Crouched thick in the entry they were seeking him, emboldened by his failure to reply. Shouts went up, calling for their mates who might be within earshot.

'There he is! Get him, boys! It's the Rio Kid!'

Blasting bullets were hunting him. Prepared to make his dash to freedom, the cool, unruffled Kid threw up both Colts and let go.

Lead ripped through the men in the door. He could see their darkish bulks against the lighter sky. Soupy Lou was still screeching, in a dither of terror. Appalled by the tearing bullets the Kid drove into them, the gunnies at the door rolled back, those who could move, and the Kid reached the opening, his hot Colts still blazing.

As he was about to jump for it, to shoot into

them at both flanks, and perhaps reach freedom, Soupy Lou's hand caught hold of his ankle. It was not bravery on the small outlaw's part but the clutch of a drowning man, reaching for anything near.

The Kid's dash was checked for precious instants that meant life or death. Griggs was so certain Pryor meant to kill him that he could not get it out of his head. He held to the Kid's boot, and Pryor was tripped as he tore free.

In a flying ball, striving desperately to regain balance, the Kid hurtled from the warehouse of his own terrific momentum, and his Colts were necessarily slow in getting to work. Instead of his smashing the gunnies with lead, they had first chance at him, and a roaring fusilade sought him as they fired.

The slugs were aimed for breast and head, but most of them sang over him as he landed flat on the dirt. But one struck and a stunning blackness came upon the Rio Kid. He did not rise from that spot.

'Is—is he dead, boys?' Soupy Lou Griggs whimpered, his teeth chattering violently.

The gunnies, around the Kid, pistols ready, were examining their captive.

'If he ain't, he soon will be,' growled one.

'I can't find no wound,' said another, bent over the prostrate Kid.

'Roll him over.'

Rough hands turned the unconscious Pryor

on his back.

'Here it is, and it's a funny one! . . . Strike another match, Blacky. Look! The slug run across his chest, so close to his heart the shock knocked him out!'

'What yuh goin' to do?' demanded Soupy Lou. He was getting back his nerve as he realized that the Kid, the man he so feared, was helpless.

'Cut his gizzard out,' growled Blacky. 'What yuh think?'

'No yuh ain't! Kansas Joe'll decide what to do with this skunk. After all, I tripped him, and he's my prisoner. The Kid savvies a lot, and I figger we can wring plenty information outa him. C'mon, pick him up and throw him in that wagon.'

The wagon with its outriders crossed Cherry Creek and swung west toward the Black Hills. It rolled on for hours until it finally turned into a deep box canyon and finally stopped before a high granite cliff. There were more wagons here, a hundred or more mustangs, and a great band of gunnies. Red fires lit the clearing in the woods, and men were hard at work, storing goods in a great cave, catching them there.

'Hey, Joe, Joe! Look what we got!'

Kansas Joe Murphy rolled over to them on his stumpy legs as Soupy Lou Griggs, with a bandage tied on his wounded hand, jumped from the back of the wagon.

'See who I captured!' boasted Lou Griggs. 'The Rio Kid hisself!'

Kansas Joe cursed, reached in, and grabbed the legs of the Rio Kid. Yanking him out, he let the wounded Kid fall heavily to earth.

'Damn' if it ain't!' he snarled. 'Got him at last! Wait'll the Chief hears this!'

The Kid was rapidly trussed, hand and foot, and carried over under a spreading cedar at one side.

Soon a warning call was heard from the canyon door, and Kansas Joe hurried that way. A man whose face was muffled by his turned-up collar, swung from a lathered, dust-covered horse.

'Hello, Joe,' he grunted.

'Howdy, Chief. Glad yuh've come. Need yore advice. Things ain't worked so well. I got yore warnin' and we cleaned the stuff outa Cherryville.'

'Then what's wrong?'

'Well,' Murphy replied, licking his thick lip nervously, 'we missed out on the massacree of a big party of immigrants under a feller named Jake Burton. There was round thirty of 'em. Everything was set, my men was in but they got away.'

'Spotted Fawn told me all that. Yuh've finished 'em off since, I expect.'

'No, suh. Spotted Fawn come in with yore letter. I had men huntin' for them Burton folks. The Rio Kid done saved 'em the fust

117

time, him and Charlie Reynolds, but my spies finally smelled 'em out again. Then up comes that Billy North hombre, and plugs two of 'em, but the third got away and reported. Chief, I hate to tell yuh, but they're at that deadwood gulch we wanted.'

'What! Yuh fool, it's worth a million and more! I need that gold to carry on! It's mine, damn yuh!'

Kansas Joe Murphy, tough as he was, quailed before the rage of the Great Chief. Cursing, raving, the Chief stormed up and down. At last he pulled himself together.

'Get after 'em, and kill 'em all, every one!' he said in a deadly tone, through gritted teeth. 'Wipe 'em out! Yuh've bungled everything, Murphy, damn yore hide, but this'll be run right now. I'll do it myself!'

'Yes, suh. But listen, Chief! I've *captured* the Rio Kid! He's here now.'

'The Kid! Curse him, he's made me a lot of trouble. I nearly got him on my way over but he's quick as a tiger. Fetch him here. I'll question him, then cut his heart out myself!'

Kansas Joe was glad to have turned the wrath of his terrible, deadly boss on the Kid. The Chief hated Bob Pryor for many reasons—the spoiling of his plans, the work the scout had done at Cherryville.

In the deep shadow, the Chief waited for his arch-foe to be brought, helpless, before him. From his pocket he drew a cigar, bit the

118

end off, and lighted up.

CHAPTER XIV

Gold Galore

Jolted awake by falling to the ground as he was unceremoniously dumped from the wagon, Bob Pryor came back to life. He was racked with pain. His entire chest felt stiff and his ears were banging. Yet he had enough control of his faculties to play possum. From beneath veiled lids he saw that there were great forces of enemies about him, and realized his utter helplessness.

Then he was roughly bound, hand and foot. Outlaws came to stare down at him curiously as he lay, still as death.

Soon a couple of huskies, one of them Kansas Joe Murphy, picked him up by wrists and ankles, and carried him away from the main camp. They went along the canyon path, turning into a grove of cottonwoods.

'Here he is, Chief,' Murphy said, dumping the limp Kid on the ground.

The Kid sought to make out the figure and features of the man Kansas Joe called Chief, but that individual stood to one side, and unless he wished to show he was awake, Pryor could not turn. It was quite dark under the

119

trees, away from the glow of the fires.

Something reached the Kid's keen nostrils —the aromatic odor of cigar smoke.

'I've smelled that before,' he thought. 'It's a funny scent—diff'rent-like.'

The Chief stepped back, and Kansas Joe followed. The low murmur of deep voices came to the Kid, mingled with sounds from the camp up the wooded canyon.

The Rio Kid, trussed hand and foot, lay about six feet from the thick-growing cottonwoods to the north of the little opening. The Chief and Kansas Joe were on the camp side. But squatted right at Pryor's head was a burly armed bandit, with his back to the trees, guarding the prisoner.

Without warning the gunny pitched forward on his face, uttering a low groan. An instant later the Rio Kid was violently jerked back into the trees.

Though the movement broke open the painful chest wound and sent waves of anguish through him, the iron-willed Kid did not cry out or make a sound.

'Ssh!' a low, tense whisper warned. 'Ees I, General!'

Celestino Mireles, lean and dark, his white teeth gleaming in his sharp-angled face, knelt by him. He drew the blood-dripping knife which he had thrust into his sash in order to pull the Kid among the trees. With the razor-sharp, foot-long blade he cut the Kid's bonds, and helped him to his feet.

'Hey, what the hell!'

Kansas Joe Murphy, engaged in deep conversation with his Chief, had glanced up, seen the collapsed guard, and the empty space where the Kid had lain a moment before.

The Mexican pushed a six-gun into the Kid's hand.

'Can you walk, General?' he whispered.

'Yeah—c'mon. Yuh got hosses?'

'Your own.'

By the exercise of sheer will power, the Kid ran after Mireles, anxiously, looking back. Shock still had him in its grip, and he had to fight to stay on his feet. Guns began banging behind them. They heard the zip of bullets in the leaves.

'Don't shoot back!' the Kid gasped. 'Only give us away!'

He thought he could go no farther, but struggled on a few more yards, trailing the lithe, slim Mexican. Celestino cut left, to the open trail in the canyon.

'They got a guard at the entrance!' warned the Kid. Mireles' white teeth flashed a grin.

'No more,' he assured.

Saber stood there, and Celestino's mustang. The Kid got hold of his saddle-horn, and the Mex, realizing how badly injured his friend was, boosted him up. Hanging low over the leather, pistol stuck in belt so he could grip with both hands, the Kid rode after his pard,

121

more dead than alive. Yells and gunshots rang behind them in the deep, dark box canyon. The pursuit was on.

They sped between towering granite sentinels. At the base of one lay a dead gunny, the guard who had been disposed of by the silent, swift-moving Mireles as he had trailed his friend to the heart of the enemy stronghold.

Celestino was delighted at having brought his partner out of death's jaw.

'I see you, General, a long way off, las' night,' he explained. 'Jus'fore ze light go. I peek up ze trail, follow to Cherryveele. But zen I hear shots. When I come up, zey have take' yuh off. But I fin' Saber, and we trail ze wagon here!'

'Nice work,' muttered the Kid, head sagging on his chest.

Mireles grew alarmed. 'General, yuh are bad hurt! Here, lean on me!'

With a mighty effort, the Kid sought to pull himself together.

'Got to make it,' he growled.

The Chief, Kansas Joe Murphy, and his hard-riding devils were spurting on their trail . . .

*   *   *

Billy North never relaxed his vigilance in the days following his arrival at the deadwood gulch, aptly named 'Deadwood' by the immigrants, when it became a camp.

There was gold, plenty of it, and the lure of it caused men to forget all danger in their desire to get it out.

The life of the camp was rough. Food consisted of fresh meat brought down by the skill of hunters, and meagre supplies of flour and coffee that were packed in. But because he could be near Edith Burton, sit with her in the cool of the evening, see her, fresh as a daisy in the morning dew, serve her and guard her, made the place a paradise for young Billy North.

Jake Burton was a fine leader, careful and good-natured. All looked up to him. The Ulman brothers, lean and dark, were pillars of strength, and Ike Ulman's wife was stout and cheerful. Uncle Dan Olliphant, Burton's chief aide, had an infectious laugh that spread among his friends, keeping them happy. His wife, Aunt Nenny, never stopped talking, but she was ever ready to nurse the sick or help out.

Calamity Jane Canary threw herself wholeheartedly into the camp life but just as she felt more at home in men's instead of women's clothing, she leaned more toward mining and hunting than toward women's work. Always calm and collected, Calamity Jane was a tower of strength.

But the main business was washing gold

from the creek or digging for it in the sandy banks of the deep, tortuous gulch.

Every evening, before dark, however, North would come in and herd them all back into the stockade on the west hill. Gates were barred and sentries set. He insisted on every precaution, though some laughed at him. The Sioux had not come near the gulch, and Deadwood camp had grown used to the threat of red danger.

'Wonder where in hell Kansas Joe's gang is?' Billy North asked himself, again and again.

He was certain that the man who had escaped, disguised as an Indian, would carry news of the Burton party back, and he was expecting Murphy's whole gang.

One afternoon, on his sentry post above the gulch, Billy North suddenly tautened, rifle coming to shoulder. He saw three riders, white men in felt Stetsons, and rough clothing, coming from the southwest.

The trio of horsemen came slowly closer and closer to North's eyrie. He was well hidden, and the depth of the gulch where the immigrants were taking out their gold, made it hard to cross, although it shallowed off to the south. North believed the approaching riders might be Murphy's scouts, but then the leader swung in his saddle, and Billy North got a good look at his face.

'Dang my hide!' exclaimed Billy North,

leaping to his feet. He started down the rocks, through the screening brush. 'Hey, Marshal!' he called.

The man on the black mount started, his hand flying to the butt of an ivory-handled six-gun, two of which he carried in his slick holsters. Then he saw who it was, and a smile spread over his face, his flowing mustache twitching in pleasure.

'Howdy, younker! What yuh doin' in these parts? Same as us I reckon?'

He thrust out a slim hand as Billy North looked up into the strong face.

'Wild Bill' Hickok was in his middle thirties, hero of a hundred shooting escapades, scout and cow-town marshal, known to every frontiersman. He was said to be the deadliest killer west of the Mississippi. North had seen him in action in Abilene and was willing to swear to Hickok's ability with pistols.

Hickok's features were pleasingly regular. He had a thin-lipped, sensitive mouth, and his heavy brown hair fell to his shoulders. His steel-blue eyes were open and frank. Now he wore a dark suit, broad-brimmed hat and fine calf-skin boots. His voice was pleasing and soft as he addressed North.

'Yeah,' he drawled. 'Meet my pards, Lew Twill and Marty O'Brien, North.'

Twill and O'Brien were run-of-the-mill Westerners, evidently prepared to do some prospecting. They wore miners' garb, and

125

miners' packs, pans, short-handled picks and shovels stuck from the packs on their led horses.

'News leaked out that there was gold inn these hills, younker,' said Wild Bill. 'We come after it. Me, I don't go in for diggin', but there are other honest ways to win it.'

Hickok winked a steely eye. He was a master of cards, a gambler by trade. Even when acting as lawkeeper in some insanely wild Frontier post, Hickok worked at the pasteboards.

Gold strikes, no matter how carefully guarded, would leak out. Billy North knew that. He hesitated, but these three were decent men, and Wild Bill Hickok was worth a dozen ordinary men in a scrap.

'I'll introduce yuh to my friends,' he said. 'They're down in the deadwood gulch.'

'Say,' observed Wild Bill, 'there's a passel of Sioux south-east of here, son. I seen fifty, sixty fires. That line of peaks blocks 'em off from here and they was distant, but Sittin' Bull and Gall are no slouches when it comes to a scrap.'

'I savvy,' North nodded. 'That's one reason I been on watch, Wild Bill. Another reason is a gang of gunnies run by one Kansas Joe Murphy!'

Wild Bill Hickok cursed sulphurously.

'That rollin' black-heart!' he exclaimed. 'I'll nail his hide to the barn wall one day. Run into the skunk in Kansas and I'm still askin' myself why I didn't plug him 'stead of lettin' him off with a jail sentence and a bang on the head.'

North led the three down into the gulch by the secret entrance. Jake Burton came from his claim at Billy North's hail, and shook hands with Hickok and his friends.

'Yuh're welcome, gents,' Burton told them. 'Plenty for all. We've staked claims. All you need do is jest observe the boundaries.'

'All right, Burton,' Hickok said. 'The boys'll get to work in the mornin'.'

'Hey, Bill!'

Hickok swung, saw Calamity Jane, grinning broadly, running toward him.

'Why, dang my pernicious hide if it ain't little Calamity! Howdy, howdy!'

CHAPTER XV

Attack

Old acquaintances on the Frontier, Hickok and Calamity Jane shook hands. Wild Bill Hickok had a terrific reputation as a fighter, and was a legendary figure all through the West.

The steely eyes swept the tortuous gulch, took in the burned black pine skeletons on the slopes.

'Huh, now I savvy why yuh called this camp Deadwood.'

Two years later he was to die at this spot, at Deadwood, shot through the back by an assassin. But of that roll of Fate's dice Wild Bill had no inkling as he had his first look at the rough little camp.

North basked for a few moments in Edith Burton's smile and had a drink. Then, stuffing some meat and hard bread into his pocket, he slid up from the narrow rock door into the gulch, returning to the high spot from which he kept his vigil.

Hardly was he in position, rifle lying by his hand, munching a mouthful of jerky beef, than he tensed, craning to stare eastward.

A great woods stretched that way, the woods through which Calamity Jane and Billy had come when they had saved Jake Burton from the fate that had overtaken Sloan. Over the woods now, birds were black specks winging in the warm air, lines of them, flying away from hidden men or animals, like waves from beaten water.

North grabbed his Sharps, watching as he started for the gulch. A low space in the trees brought him a startingly bright scintillation, sunlight on metal.

Scuttling to warn his friends, Billy had almost reached the rock gate when, looking back over his shoulder, he saw a line of painted, befeathered riders emerging from the woods. They swept toward him, headed straight for Deadwood Gulch.

In the lead was a burly giant in buckskin and an eagle feather headdress. His face was smeared with wide streaks of red, yellow and blue stains—war-paint. Beside him rode a squat, short-legged man, and in this bright light North could see the smear of a wiry black beard, despite attempts to paint over it.

'That's Kansas Joe, shore enough,' grunted North.

Then the oncoming riders glimpsed him. The big leader's gun flew up, and a hundred more followed suit. North jumped for the protecting granite and made it in the nick of time, for bullets smacked like hail on the stone, spattering him with fragments of rock and lead.

'To the stockade, folks!' roared North, his strong voice echoing in the tortuous gulch. 'They're a-comin'!'

Then he ran back, as he saw the alarm had been heard, and began shooting up at the great killer mob driving on him. His Sharps roared its throaty, heavy voice of death. A man flew from his barebacked mustang, lay quiet.

He had hoped to pick off Kansas Joe or the burly leader, but they had swerved south. No doubt they knew of a way down the steep side.

Billy North's slugs annoyed the attacking riders, singing close to rapid-moving bodies, tearing flesh and bone. Bunches of gunnies galloped full tilt in the wake of their leaders, and with his aim never shaken North's Sharps exploded in his steady hands.

He got four, then they hit the screen of brush and sharp rocks along the lip of the twisting ravine. A dozen swung over to finish him. He wounded one, then started to retreat.

His friends were all across the creek, on their way up the slope, cutting through the burned woods to reach the stockade. The men on the east lip of the gulch threw themselves from their horses and, grabbing rifles, began firing after them, with Kansas Joe bellowing commands above the din of smashing guns.

North fell back, splashing across the stream, taking to the trees in the nick of time as his foes oozed through the gap. Sheltered by a wide tree trunk, he paused to shoot back.

Scattered shots sounded from above him, to the west. Up there Wild Bill Hickok, with Calamity Jane and O'Brien flanking him, coolly picked off the visible foe, making stands as they retreated.

Billy North was halfway up to the stockade, and his friends were pouring into it. He was just congratulating himself on his foresight and watchfulness, when through the heavy volleying gunfire he heard a woman crying:

'Jake! Jake!'

'Edith get back there!' he cried, but she either did not hear or was too determined to find her uncle to turn.

The girl was running downhill, toward the gulch, and a moment later the cursing North, working over as rapidly as he could for the tripping underbrush, saw Burton scramble out of the trap and leg it up the slope for the trees. He had a canvas bag clutched in one hand.

Thick behind him, not more than a couple of hundred yards off, bunched the gunnies. They were now dismounted, and had rifles steadied on flat rock tops behind which they had taken cover.

North caught the glint of a dozen carbine barrels in the sunlight. He threw his heavy Sharps to shoulder and sent a .50-caliber, eight-to-the-pound ball smashing among them. But they let go almost in unison an instant later.

Jake Burton whirled, staggered a few steps, and fell on his face, his arms stretched toward the stockade.

His niece screamed with shrill horror over the pounding din of battle. She was frantic, for she loved her uncle as a parent. He had brought her up from childhood when her mother and father had been killed by Indians on a westward trek. She ran on, and knelt over Burton, seeking to raise him.

Wild Bill and Calamity Jane, seeing the girl below, turned and then started toward her, and Billy North was almost there. Bullets were hailing into the woods, and women screamed as they saw Edith's danger.

Blind to everything save his sweetheart's peril, North dashed ahead full tilt, hopping fallen trees, driving on through thickets. He reached her, but a whizzing, singing slug struck her and she fell across the body of Jake Burton.

'C'mon up, North!' bawled Hickok.

His ivory-handled Colts were banging into the murderous foe across the gulch. Calamity Jane Canary, in her frontiers-man's buckskin pants and jacket, was shooting alongside her friend, Wild Bill.

'Edith Edith!' gasped North brokenly, stooping to raise her limp body.

A glance told him that Jake Burton was dead. A heavy bullet had struck his brain-pan and he had died as he fell, riddled by enemy lead. In his outstretched hand he clutched a canvas bag, his collection of gold. He kept it near him as he worked, North knew, had started out of the gulch without it at the alarm, then gone back to get it. For the yellow lure he had died, like so many adventurous and courageous men.

Wild Bill, Calamity Jane, and several others concentrated heavy fire upon the group of attackers immediately facing the spot where Billy North ran, carrying his sweetheart. Bullets smacked into the bush-fringed rocks across the gulch, seeking to keep the killers down until North could reach the stockade.

He had about fifty yards to go, and was almost in the trees when a slug bit a chunk from his left arm. He paid no attention to the wound, but drove on, making the woods where he could find cover behind which to retreat.

The stockade gate was held open and, supported by Wild Bill and Calamity, Billy North staggered into the enclosure. His mouth was drawn to a taut line of agony, and terror for his loved one was tearing his heart as though it had been ripped by a sharp knife.

'Ev'rybody in bar the gates!' ordered Hickok. 'Man them loopholes, boys.'

Wild Bill was coolly taking charge of the defense. An expert in all sorts of warfare, Hickok knew just what to do.

Inside the stockade were jars and casks of water, and every canteen was filled. There were food supplies, ammunition and spare weapons, blankets and rude shelters. Loopholes that were slits from the outside, and widening as they pierced the thick palings, so that the defender could manipulate his rifle and yet be little exposed, had been made at strategic points. Under Hickok's direction, the first-line fighters took these stands. The youngsters and women broke out ammunition and spare weapons, loading and assisting.

Billy North, his eyes wide with anguish, but fighting to hold his emotions in check, laid his sweetheart gently on a blanket spread by Aunt Nenny.

'Where—where's she hit?' he said hoarsely. 'Calamity—Calamity, please come help!'

Martha Jane Canary, expert at nursing and taking care of gunshot cases, relinquished her loophole to a man and came over, stooping beside North.

Blood stained Edith's calico dress, over her left ribs.

'I'll take charge of her,' Calamity said. 'You get on and fight, Billy.'

'Here they come!' came a shout.

'Hold yore fire, boys, till they're right close!' Wild Bill commanded, his voice calm and steady.

They were pioneers, these folks. For the adventure of gold they had risked all possessions and lives. Now they were paying the toll the yellow metal takes.

There was no panic in the stockade. The women and youths were calm, ready to help to the end. Billy North's foresight in building the stockade gave them a good chance, despite the odds of three to one against them.

The enemy had dismounted, and were coming across Deadwood Gulch, snaking up around to reach the woods from which they might approach the stockade. The firing had lulled for the moment, as Kansas Joe got his gunnies into position.

'Ringin' us for a charge, boys,' announced Wild Bill. 'Jest hold till they start in.'

The figures in Indian disguise crept through

the woods. The defenders hardly saw any of the enemy for twenty long minutes. Then suddenly from all sides heavy rifle fire opened up. Bullets smacked into the sturdy intertwined poles of the stockade or sang menacingly overhead.

A horde of painted men sprang up, shooting as they came, charging for the palings.

'Now!'

Hickok gave the word, and a concerted volley of rifles banged from the palisade loopholes.

The withering, deadly fire hit half a dozen of the rapidly running gunnies. Three did not rise, and the others crawled back to shelter.

Again the pioneers let go, and more of the foe felt the accurate lead.

The ring broke, and the men forming it scampered off for cover, unable to face the guns of the men in the stockade.

Hickok waited for half an hour. Time dragged on, and nothing came save scattered shots from the trees.

'They've had a bellyful of straight chargin',' he growled. 'Git a drink and some rest, gents. We'll be busy tonight.'

Only one man in the stockade had been hit. His cheek had been torn by a bullet which had found its way through his loophole.

North, who had steeled himself to do his duty to defend the stockade, now swung and with agonized appeal in his eyes sought the round face of Calamity Jane who squatted close by Edith Burton.

'What—what is it?' he asked.

'She'll be all right, I'm shore, Billy,' Calamity told him cheerfully.

But North knew the woman was lying, and his heart felt paralyzed.

'Where's she hit?' he demanded roughly. 'Tell me!'

'Aw, Billy—bullet cut in close to her heart,' Calamity said hesitantly.

'You get it out?'

'No, I ain't. And I ain't goin' to try. It'd take a real saw-bones to do it without killin' her.'

'A sawbones! Where we goin' to get a doctor?'

North gave a mirthless laugh, more terrible than a sob.

Calamity Jane shrugged, watching his tortured young face. North guessed, without being informed, that Edith had little chance to live unless she had expert medical care.

Night was close at hand. The western sky was red as the sun went down behind the Black Hills, the mighty, unknown wilderness of the Sioux.

Gold now was as nothing. No amount of gold could buy life—the lives of the small group in the stockade.

The black blanket of night fell over them, and the call of birds, the chirping of insects, rose on the cooling wind. Thousands of rustlings came from the woods, unnaturally loud to the strained ears of the people besieged by a cruel, relentless foe.

For an hour they waited, tensely, for attack. The enemy could creep in much closer under cover of dark.

'Get them water buckets ready,' ordered Hickok, and the word was passed.

His keen ears had caught something out there that was different from the other myriad night sounds.

Suddenly dozens of giant fireflies sprang into being. Red-dish, smoky flames were flitting through the trees toward the stockade.

These were brands to be thrown in on the people inside the stockade to smoke them out.

'Aim fire!'

Hickok's commanding voice gave the order, and a dozen of the fireflies fell to earth, flickering out. Others came hurtling into the stockade, but the women and children, with buckets of water and wet blankets, quickly put out the blazing torches.

Wild slugs rapped the palisades. The full night attack was on!

CHAPTER XVI

Night Melee

Minutes dragged like hours. Coolheaded men now had charge in the stockade, and if no more reinforcements joined the enemy ranks they might hold out for a long while.

But Billy North was aware that the longer they had to hold out, the nearer Edith would come to death.

The stars overhead were shut off and on by scudding banks of dark clouds driven by a strong southwest wind. In one of those faintly lighted moments Wild Bill Hickok, at ease by his loophole, clicked his ivory-handled Colt to full cock and took aim through the port.

'Somebody sneakin' up,' he whispered.

But the next instant, as he heard a low voice from outside, his gun hand dropped to his side, and he uttered a low ejaculation of surprise.

'Don't shoot!' he heard a man's voice say, in a rasped whisper. 'It's the Rio Kid! Open the gate for me!'

Wild Bill peered keenly through the loophole and recognized the Rio Kid who, with keen ears tuned to every sound, was pressed flat against the earth close outside the stockade.

A couple of day's rest had done wonders for Bob Pryor, and his iron constitution had thrown off the shock of the wound sustained in Cherryville. Under Celestino Mireles' care he had rapidly regained his power. Saber, picked up outside the camp of Kansas Joe on Cherry Creek, by the Mexican who had saved Pryor from torture death at the hands of Murphy's relentless Chief, had been rested. He had carried the Kid's saddle-bags, carbine, and spare pistols.

After eluding the foe in the darkness they had ridden up on a heavily bushed ridge, in deep woods, westward in the Black Hills. They had camped there to let the Kid recuperate.

Ever alert, they had later spied the riding band led by Kansas Joe Murphy at a distance. The burly feathered Chief and Spotted Fawn were with them, all galloping full-speed westward.

'Now where they headin'?' growled Pryor. 'Look like they're up to mischief!'

From Mireles he had learned that Billy North and Calamity Jane had headed into the Hills on the trail of Burton's folks. That had given the Kid an idea of where the Murphy band were headed.

Saddling up, Mireles and his 'General' had taken the trail of the large gang of disguised gunnies. For miles they had stuck on the fresh sign. Then the Kid had slowed, dismounted and picked up something from the grass.

'What ees?' asked Mireles.

'Cheroot butt!' The Kid sniffed and chewed a bit of the tobacco leaf. 'Huh, that's him! Kansas Joe's Chief! I whiffed that queer smellin' tobacco back at the canyon where yuh saved me, Celestino! And it's sorta familiar.'

Mounting they then had ridden on. The Kid had wanted to keep track of Murphy's gang for Custer, and he had a good hunch that the gunnies might be riding on the trail of the Burton party whom North had joined.

At a distance the two had trailed. From a high point, miles eastward, they had watched the first attack on Deadwood Gulch. By the time they had drawn closer in, the pioneers had been in the stockade, and the Kid and the young Mexican had settled down to wait until darkness fell.

Then the Kid, leaving the horses hidden deep in the woods with the Mexican, had started a snakelike crawl through the enemy lines. And he had won through. Now he was at the gate of the stockade.

Wild Bill Hickok unbarred the gate, and opened it a crack. The Kid crawled through the opening, rose up before them. His clothing was torn, covered by dirt, stick ends, and bits of rubble picked up by his progress, inch by inch, through the gunny bunch.

'Howdy, Kid,' Hickok said, gripping his hand. 'Ain't seen yuh since that little fuss in Abilene!'

'Evenin', Kid!' Calamity Jane cried. 'Nice place to come visitin'!'

'Is Billy North here, too?' asked Pryor.

'Yeah, here I am, Kid.' North's voice was hoarse from strain.

'His little lady's hurt bad, Kid,' Calamity whispered. 'Bullet close to the heart. Can't get it, and it's affectin' her bad. Breathin's awful ragged. We need a real sawbones.'

The Rio Kid learned then of Jake Burton's death, and of what had happened since he had last seen North and his friends.

'Reckon yuh savvy them lobos out there are disguised whites, Bill,' he said to Hickok.

'That's what North figgered, Kid,' replied Wild Bill.

'They're Kansas Joe Murphy's gunnies, fixed up like Sioux, ridin' under a dirty hombre I mean to exterminate one of these days,' growled Pryor. 'Him and me got a bone to pick —a whole skeleton if yuh ask me.'

He was boiling mad at the insidious, hidden killer who had caused so much horror in the Black Hills country. To this man he ascribed the frame-up against himself which had occurred at the Fort, and many other deadly attempts.

'Thing to do,' Pryor went on, having thought the situation over with his keen, strategic mind, 'is to bust them murderers and do it quick. We can't sit in here and run outa water and food, boys.'

The silent circle of fighters grouped about him sought the keen, handsome face of the ace scout and frontiersman, the Rio Kid.

'However, it's three to one out there, Kid,' reminded Wild Bill, 'and we're countin' younkers and women at that!'

'Yeah, but the line of them attackers is thin on the west, which is how I come through. They're camped down there in a hidden spot, half of 'em, while the rest stand guard. I was within twenty-five yards of 'em. That's where they got their horses now, and grub. They got to eat and rest, and their Chief's keepin' half of 'em on duty, half off.'

'Huh!' Wild Bill got a glimmering of the Kid's reckless plan, interestedly listening as Pryor elaborated.

'I want five men with me,' the Kid continued. 'We'll hit that camp, and hit her hard.'

'Good!' agreed Hickok. 'That's the stuff. Give me a quick scrap every time.'

'Me, too,' chimed in Calamity. 'Count me one, Kid.'

'Yuh better stick here, Calamity,' Pryor said.

'Huh!' Martha Jane said indignantly. 'I'm a-goin', boys, if I have to go alone! Make up yore minds to that.'

Nothing could dissuade her. In the dim light of the stockade, Pryor got his volunteers. They were Wild Bill Hickok, Calamity, Billy

North, the lean, dark-faced Ben Ulman, and Hickok's miner friend Marty O'Brien.

Hatless, and with their feet cased in soft moccasins, so that no leather could creak and betray them in their desperate enterprise, the six made ready for the sortie.

At the signal, several stones were hurled into the wood on the east side of the stockade, rattling down the slope. This was a drawoff, as the half dozen picked fighters were boosted over the sharp palings on the west flank and crawled for the woods, with the Kid in the lead.

It was close going, from rock to rock, from bush to bush. Each one was an accomplished woodsman and stalker, and the brilliant Kid who was leading them was a genius at such work.

Almost in his ear, Bob Pryor heard a man clear his throat. He froze. He could see the sentinel, with a rifle between his knees, squatted facing the stockade.

Wraiths in the night, seeking to break the enemy and escape before the hordes of Sioux should discover them and come in, aware that Edith Burton's life depended on the ability to get her expert surgical assistance quickly, the half dozen daring fighters, awaited the Kid's decision. An alarm now would mean the ruin of their hopes, death to some, or all of the six.

The Kid's hand clutched the bowie-knife in his sash. He left the ground with the unerring spring of a panther. An arm like a steel band encircled the startled gunny's throat, choking off his gasping cry. The knife drove deep, and a moment later the Kid crept on, followed by his companions.

Several hundred yards on, west of the stockade, and down the rocky, bushed slope, a grove of dark pines rose in splendor to the wilderness sky.

By hand signals, the Kid disposed his six about this grove. In the faint light, shut on and off as the black clouds struck the slice of moon, their keen eyes saw the blanketed, silent figures of men, sleeping in the circle.

Guns up, the six took aim.

'Fire!' shrieked the Rio Kid.

Colts at close range roared in the night, accurately pouring leaden death into the gunnies. The banging echoes ran through the hills, and the shrieks of startled men joined the din.

As fast as he could shoot, the Kid stung the murderous gang with his slugs. They were leaping up, reaching for their weapons, and ragged replying volleys sought the flashes of the attackers.

Skillfully, because every one of them was an ace at gun-fighting, the six men from the stockade obeyed the Kid's orders. Relentlessly they shot in on the massed gunnies.

Confused shouts, screams for help arose from the grove. A bunch tore into the pines

144

toward the horses that were dancing and stamping at their tethers.

'Give it to 'em boys!' bawled the Kid, guns spitting hot lead.

Slugs from deadly six-guns sought the flesh of Kansas Joe Murphy's evil killers.

Hunting for the Chief and Murphy, the Rio Kid flitted from tree trunk to tree trunk. The rapidly fired guns had taken a terrific toll of the gang, which had been snoozing in the grove. At least half of them had been hit. Suddenly, as the survivors split off in every direction, some escaping by sheer weight of numbers from the death trap, the Kid came face to face with a grotesque bowlegged figure.

'Murphy!' he howled.

An instant later, as the moon cast its silvery light through the clouds on the scene, Kansas Joe threw up his six-shooter. 'Damn yore soul, Rio Kid!' he bellowed.

The immense torso above the foreshortened, crooked legs was a target the Kid could not miss. Kansas Joe, aware of what he was up against in facing Bob Pryor, knowing the man's speed and accurate ability with a gun, dared not wait. He fired quickly, instantly.

And yet, though speed was essential, it was the man who took his time—that necessary second-breath a cool brain and coordinated muscles needed—who could make the first shot count. The Kid felt the burning path of Kansas Joe's bullet as it grooved the flesh of his thigh. Then his own Colt roared, like an echo to Murphy's.

Kansas Joe's ugly, bearded head snapped back. The heavy body no longer remained supported on the bent legs, but quivered. He collapsed on the carpet of pine needles.

The Kid sprang toward him. Kansas Joe was gone. A bluish hole was between his red-rimmed, ugly eyes.

Lieutenants were roaring orders to the remainder of the gunmen. The lines around the stockade broke up, rushing back to help thcir attacked comrades.

'Back!' the Kid called to Wild Bill. 'Let's get outa here! The whole lot of 'em'll converge on us in a minute.'

Bodies lay in blankets, or heaped in the pine grove. Horses were stampeding, fought by cursing, furious outlaws. Bullets were rattling thick as gunny leaders forced their hireling fighters toward the center of the disturbance.

The Kid and his friends faded back, shooting a way past the thin forces of the foe that ran toward them through trees and bush. The bedlam was frightful, as gunshots and harsh curses arose in a mad din.

They cut over toward the stockade, piercing the enemy line, smashed by the alarm. The gate was opened and they piled through.

Back inside, bleeding from gashes, but with none of them seriously wounded, the six threw themselves down, panting for breath, Water was brought them. Calamity Jane, face blackened by powder and dirt, and a trickle of blood showing on her hand from an arm wound, grinned at the Kid.

'Yuh shore think up excitin' plays, Kid,' she complimented.

Pryor smiled as he got up and went to the gate, listening. He could hear the crashing of brush below, where the shaken gunnies were milling as they fought.

'That oughta discourage 'em for awhile,' he remarked. 'I savvy that sort. They don't like it too tough. Reckon that Chief of theirs will have trouble gettin' 'em back into action after they count their dead.'

'Yuh're right, Kid,' agreed Hickok. 'They won't hold out long.'

CHAPTER XVII

'The Sioux Are Here'

Cursing, the Great Chief rounded up his killers in the woods. In the pine grove clearing, the dead lay as they had fallen under the guns of the Rio Kid and his fighting crew.

The Chief had been out on the line. The

sleeping gang had been under Kansas Joe.

The burly Chief, in his Sioux getup, the feather headdress dangling down his stooped back, turned Kansas Joe over, staring at the ugly countenance.

'Through the brain,' he growled, his teeth gritting in fury. ' 'Twas that Rio Kid, Chief,' chattered Soupy Lou. 'Lucky for me I was hid under a fallen pine and they missed me!'

'Shut up! How many got it?'

'Twenty-two, Chief! Gawd, it's awful! That Kid's a demon. I ain't pinin' to fight him no longer!' Terror made Soupy Lou Griggs rash enough to speak so to his boss.

The Chief swung, seized him by the throat with a powerful hand, lifted him from the earth, and shook him as a terrier shakes a rat. Soupy Lou squeaked for mercy. He fell to his knees as the Great Chief released him and kicked him with a spurred boot.

'Damn yore yeller soul, Griggs!' snarled the Chief. 'I'll wring yore craw to the end next time, savvy? Shut up that quittin' talk.'

'He's right,' a gunny lieutenant said sullenly. 'Killin' like that'll finish us. I ain't goin' against that stockade no more. Damned if I do.'

The mutiny spread swiftly. They had lost over a third of their number in the attack, and in the Kid's ambush.

The Chief's painted face was black with fury, but he knew the sort of men with whom

148

he had to deal. With the odds in their favor, they would kill. But hirelings that they were, the might of the Rio Kid smote them with fright.

'That Deadwood Gulch is mine,' the Great Chief snapped. Swinging, he called: 'Spotted Fawn!'

The lean renegade Sioux came forward, moving with the grace of a tiger. His high-boned face, hawk beak showing his pride, fixed the Great Chief, awaiting instructions.

'Yes, Great Chief! Spotted Fawn is here!'

The Chief picked half a dozen gunnies whom he considered stronger than the common run.

'Grab the fastest hosses, and come on, pronto,' the Chief commanded. 'Hagen, pull the men back, and jest try to hold the stockaders inside in case they try to escape. We'll be back by dawn.'

'All right, Chief,' Hagen growled.

Led by the Chief, the six, with Spotted Fawn at the boss' side, rode hell-for-leather southward, passing through the mountain range by way of a narrow gap.

They bore east, riding madly in the night wind. It was a hard, long run but their mustangs were sturdy and swift.

The Sioux village stood on the river bank, and as they approached it the evil-eyed Chief peered down at the tepees. Guardian warriors stood about the village, before dying fires, sentinels against possible enemy raiders. The Sioux had hereditary foes such as Rees and Crows, always anxious to strike and run off horses and loot when they saw a chance.

'It's up to you, Spotted Fawn,' the Great Chief growled.

'Get ready.'

He raised his carbine, taking aim at the silent bronzed sentry framed against the river bank. The white men with him followed suit, picking off others of the Sioux.

Spotted Fawn, on his paint pony, cut through the trees down toward the village. The five rifles in the hands of the men he had left suddenly barked, and three Sioux warriors fell to earth. Another felt stinging lead that tore through his brawny shoulder.

Yells of alarm arose, and Sioux warriors rushed from tepees, like disturbed ants from a great hill. Warwhoops crackled in the wilderness air as Indians fought back.

'That oughta do it,' snarled the Great Chief. 'C'mon, boys, let's ride!'

Swinging his mustang, he galloped back on the trail the way they had come, to Deadwood.

But Spotted Fawn kept going. As he neared the Sioux village, he sang out in his native tongue. Lashing his paint horse, lathered and bleeding from spur gouges, and riding low over the silky yellow mane, Spotted Fawn galloped up to Chief Sitting Bull.

Chief Gall, the Sioux Napoleon, military

leader of the great Nation, Red Cloud, and other famous leaders of the red men were standing in a bunch, surrounded by armed warriors. There were over a thousand Sioux in the village, swarming about their fallen friends.

Spotted Fawn threw himself from his pony, dashed to Gall and Sitting Bull.

'The *wasichus* did this!' he cried in Sioux. 'I saw them with my own eyes! Five of them, from the Deadwood Gulch, northwest of our village! They are there, many of them, taking our gold!'

Fury showed in the black eyes of the Sioux chieftains.

'Fight!' grunted Gall.

Sitting Bull leaped to the back of a powerful horse.

'Come on, Dakotas!' he shouted. 'Ride, and never return until every *wasichu* in the Black Hills is dead!'

Riding at the head of their powerful, well-armed forces, Gall and Sitting Bull, Red Cloud and other chiefs followed Spotted Fawn, hunting blood revenge, the right of the Sioux . . .

The damp, cool dawn came over the stockade, and the Rio Kid, rousing from his catnap, came instantly alert. Guards were round, tired-eyed men who had watched through the hours.

No further attack had come from the

151

enemy. The smashing of their force by the Kid's strategy had evidently stopped them.

'They're all gone, Kid,' reported Uncle Dan Olliphant. 'Reckon yuh sorta discouraged 'em last night.'

Under a shelter, covered by blankets, lay the inert form of Edith Burton. Her face was pale as flour, and the women watched over her closely. Not yet had she recovered consciousness. The bullet near her heart was slowly weakening her.

Billy North huddled as close as he could get. He had fallen into a nightmare sleep, from sheer exhaustion.

The Kid was troubled. His ear had been to the ground as he catnapped. He listened again, then vaguely he heard slight tremors.

'What the hell!' he muttered. 'Sounds like an army comin'.' He arose and went to the gate. About him stretched sleepers, some of them wounded, as he peeked from a loophole. But he could not see any of the foe in the shadows of the surrounding woods.

The light was growing stronger. Soon the sun would redden the eastern sky. Uneasy, warned of approaching danger by his alert hearing, and by some sixth sense developed by expert frontiersmen, the Kid could not keep still. The scarred flesh of an old war wound over his ribs itched, a sure sign of trouble.

He could dimly see through a vista of trees, down toward Deadwood Gulch, and the sweep of the slope beyond.

And as again he looked from a port a tide of rising war bonnets broke into sight, men riding full tilt toward the gulch and the stockade with its worn, battered crew.

'Sitting Bull! Gall! Spotted Fawn! Red Cloud!'

The Kid counted the men with the Indian leaders as they came, and then lost count.

Hundreds on hundreds of mighty warriors in full war-paint and regalia, armed with fine carbines, and with ammunition belts slung from their shoulders, swarmed into view. Hairy mustangs crowded each other as the red men sought to ride in the van for the battle.

'Up, every man!' shouted the Rio Kid. 'The Sioux are here!'

With their anger already high against the *wasichus* because of the rapid encroachment on their land, and now infuriated by the killings which had been laid to those in the stockade, the Sioux sent war-whoops into the bright morning air.

They came galloping to Deadwood Gulch, threw themselves from hairy mustangs and, with carbines in their hands, started across the creek into the woods, headed for the little group of whites on the hill.

Chief Gall, a strategist of the first order, was in charge of the attack. Sitting Bull, a medicine man, was a spiritual leader of the Sioux, while Gall, Red Cloud and others were military chiefs.

The Kid, observing the rapid approach of the swarming foes upon the battered garrison, realized at once that there was no hope of holding off such a force for long. Cool and collected, showing nothing to discourage the handful in the enclosure, he swiftly manned the loopholes for the defense. There could be no surrender. The Indians would kill them all in their fury.

To other eyes than those of men and women who knew that cruel torture-death was upon them, the red men's gorgeous barbaric appearance would have been enthralling. Strong, lithe bronzed bodies were clad in soft deerskin, elaborately ornamented in handsome patterns by squaw labor with vari-colored beads red, yellow, green, blue, every hue. The braves wore beautifully made leggings of hide, or buffalo chaps, and trimmed jackets. Some had buffalo horns or animal skulls attached to their headbands, others wore two or three eagle feathers, testifying to the number of enemies killed in battle, while many sported full headdresses of golden eagle plumes. Dried human scalps flapped at belts.

Various warrior societies Bear, Fox, Panther were represented. Standard bearers with raised feathered staffs indicated the different fighting bands. Many warriors had plastrons of drilled bone, or looped chains of bone discs on their breasts. Fortunes in pelts carelessly decorated the savages, the finest furs in the country.

Yet the beauty of the savage pageantry did not appeal to the handful of whites in the stockade. To them it meant only red death, and a torture finish for those not killed in the fight.

Wild Bill Hickok, Calamity Jane, Uncle Dan Olliphant, the Ulman brothers, and the rest of the fighting men stood ready at the ports. There was no panic. Billy North quietly loaded his Sharps from a pocket crammed with bullets. Every man there knew that if the Sioux came through the women must be shot before allowing them to fall into red hands as captives.

'Spotted Fawn roused 'em, I reckon,' mused the Kid as, carbine ready in his hands, he peeked at the tide of Sioux starting up at them. 'The white Chief's faded with his hombres. He's leavin' the Sioux to clean us out for him!'

Shrill war-whoops, the opening fire of the Indians, started. The Kid braced himself for the shock of the attack.

'Make it good, boys!' he ordered coolly. 'We got to stop that first charge.'

CHAPTER XVIII

Desperate Gamble

Knowing Indian strategy, the Rio Kid knew the importance of checking the initial rush of the braves. Foolhardy frontal assault was not considered very good strategy by Gall and other Indian military experts. They preferred the surprise, the swift blow to catch the enemy unawares.

Bob Pryor and the handful of entrapped men and women in the stockade could both see and hear the Indian chiefs giving their commands. The warriors spread swiftly into a wide circle, ringing the hill on which the stockade stood among its protective rocks. They slowly started up, crouched, guns ready, tomahawks catching the glint of the rising sun. Beady black eyes fixed the sharpened palings of the stockade behind which determined and vastly outnumbered whites waited.

Closer and closer came the Sioux, thick as leaves in the forest, then red bodies glistening with animal grease.

'Aim!' the Kid ordered quietly.

Defending rifles rose to the loopholes.

Gall shrilled a command to his braves, and the Sioux leaped up, shouting as they charged.

'Fire!' the Kid bawled.

The burst of guns sent bullets pointblank into the seething mass of Indians. Braves took lead, falling under the crush of those following.

A heavy volley spattered against the tough, thick wood of the stockade. Hurled stones and hatchets descended inside.

Shooting now as fast as they could load, with the women and children crouched behind them, making ready fresh weapons, the whites ripped the Sioux with their bullets.

Shrieks and cries of defiance mingled with the roar of hundreds of guns. The charging Sioux came to the very face of the palisades, seeking to leap up and land inside.

Strewn outside were Indian dead and wounded. Several in the stockade had received fresh wounds, but their protection was good. Fierce, painted Indian faces, grimacing to throw terror into the heart of the *wasichus,* appeared above the palings. Tomahawks and knives were raised. Six-shooters flew to action, as Wild Bill, Calamity Jane, the Kid and the other men inside the stockade fired with the rapidity of grim and deadly desperation.

White men tangled hand-to-hand with the Sioux who managed to get to the top of the fence. Women were shooting with the men now, and the young lads, too, fought for their lives.

For minutes it was nip-and-tuck. Once the

swarm overran the stockade there would be no hope.

Dead ringed the square enclosure outside. Sioux leaped over the bodies of their fallen comrades in order to get over the fence.

Blasting guns ripped them, carbine and pistol. And when it seemed hopeless to climb over the stockade fence the Indians suddenly stopped charging, turned and scuttled back into the woods.

Gall would not pay such a toll. He had ordered his braves off.

As they retreated, the Indians picked up their dead and injured, carrying them off.

'Hold it, boys!' gasped the Kid, panting from the savage, terrific battle. 'Let 'em go!'

Weary men and women threw themselves down, to regain breath, to quiet their thumping hearts. Death had held them for a time, only to let them go.

Clouds of acrid powder-smoke rose slowly from the stockade. The Sioux, squatting down in the trees and rocks below, sent long-range shots over the palings or thudding into them.

Inside, water was passed, and wounds bandaged. The Rio Kid took stock of his forces. Uncle Dan had a bad one through the shoulder, but never stopped grinning cheerfully as his injury was cauterized and bound. Others had more or less serious hurts bullet holes or slashes. Two were dead.

The Kid looked over the water supply. He

figured they had enough for about three days.

'What yuh think, Kid?' asked Hickok, keeping his voice low.

The Kid shrugged. 'They won't make a daylight charge again, that's a cinch,' he replied. 'Gall and Sitting Bull don't fancy that sorta slaughter. We took ten to one, I figger.'

'Yeah, we can hold out but for what?'

The Rio Kid did not answer that one. He saw Billy North's powder-stained, grim face, aged suddenly to hopelessness. It was not for himself, though, but for his wounded sweetheart that North felt so, the Kid understood. Caught in the stockade, Edith Burton would slowly die.

Over Deadwood Gulch, rich with Sioux gold, hung the red haze of death.

For doughty fighters such as those in the stockade, the Indians would entertain only a high respect. They loathed cowards. A scalp such as Wild Bill's or the Rio Kid's would be prized and exhibited, and the killing boasted of by the lucky brave who got his coup stick first on such a mighty foe.

Down below the Sioux began a pow-wow. Leaping, dancing warriors shouted, while the chiefs consulted.

Then the Sioux sat down to wait. There was plenty of game in the forests, and the people in the stockade could hold out only so long. In time water would be gone, and ammunition exhausted. Gall would have them without losing hundreds of his men.

'Take charge, Bill,' said the Kid. 'I'm goin' to snooze.'

Hickok nodded. A skeleton watch manned the loopholes, while worn and battered survivors sought rest. So weary were they that they slept instantly, once their heads were down.

The Rio Kid curled up in a blanket and was quickly asleep . . .

He awoke with the sunset. The stockade was quiet. All around them outside were the Sioux, patiently awaiting their moment. Gall and Sitting Bull were sure of their prey. A feast was starting, and ceremonial dances in which individual braves might boast of their exploits in the morning battle.

Red sentinels were posted, silent and austere, at strategic points to cut off any attempt to escape.

Refreshed by sleep, the Kid swallowed a little water and had a quick meal. He checked his pistols, and tied a band about his chestnut-haired head. Moccasins were on his feet. and he thrust his guns and knife into a tight sash at his slim waist.

Wild Bill Hickok watched these preparations silently. He winked as the Kid caught his eye.

'I'm goin' out at dark,' Pryor told him. 'Yuh'll be in charge, Bill.'

'Wish yuh luck,' drawled Hickok, as

lounging on his side, head in hand, he nodded.

The Kid knew as well as Wild Bill how slim was the chance of creeping through the red men. However, it was the only thing to do, the only way to instil even remote hope in the hearts of the pioneers in the stockade.

As the sky darkened suddenly, the Kid looked speculatively into the heavens. Over the heart of the mighty hills a dense rolling cloud appeared, rapidly coming upon them in the last glint of day.

Terrific flashes of lightning played about Harney's Peak, visible for miles in every direction. One of the startling thunderstorms for which the Hills were famous was making up.

Night fell upon them. The stars were shut off, but the world was lighted for seconds intermittently by vivid flashes in the sky. Thunder boomed ominously in the Black Hills as the storm rolled down upon them. Electric blue and yellow light smote them, eerie, changing the glimpsed world to an unfamiliar scene.

'Gimme a boost, Bill,' the Kid ordered.

Wild Bill Hickok stepped to the rear of the stockade.

'Yuh musta been born with a rabbit's foot in yore paw, Kid,' he muttered. 'This storm'll keep the Sioux quiet if anything will!'

These terrific manifestations of natural power awed the Sioux. Sitting Bull and other medicine men would be busy seeking to propitiate the gods of the Black Hills.

The Kid waited as a long streak of lightning flashed in the sky. As pitch darkness descended again, and the thunder rolled through the mountains, Hickok pressed his hand, and boosted him to the top of the palings. The Kid fell lightly outside and scuttled for his first bit of cover, flattening out when the next chain lightning came.

The Sioux would not think of attacking in such a storm. Their superstitious, savage hearts would be appalled.

Inching along in the dark spells, freezing flat on the ground during the lightning flashes, the Rio Kid crept down the slope from the stockade, parallel with Deadwood Gulch.

The rain began when he was about two hundred yards away. The heavens slit open and water poured out, so heavily that the Kid was soaked through in a few seconds, beaten by the large drops that battered the world. A high wind drove the storm, and drowned out what faint sounds the Kid made as he progressed.

The weird storm lasted for half an hour, during which Bob Pryor, in his desperate gamble to find some help for the besieged party of whites in the stockade, crept through the huddled Sioux sentries and swung down to the gulch.

The creek was swollen by the rain, roaring

in its rocky walls. He lay flat on the bush-fringed western lip of the ravine, waiting for one of the intermittent flashes to show him his way.

They were growing more distant. The thunder was grumbling in the distance as the storm receded from the center of the Black Hills.

There came a streak of lightning and the Kid saw that before him the cliff was straight up and down, too steep to scale. But to his left, fifty yards away, the wall had crumbled to a shale slide that was negotiable on foot.

But at the head of this slide, blocking him from crossing to the east side of the gulch and the woods where he had left Celestino Mireles hidden with Saber, stood a bronzed, silent Indian.

'Spotted Fawn!' he muttered, recognizing the lean, dark-faced renegade.

Then the illumination from the sky was shut off, plunging the world into blackness. He could hear the rushing waters of the stream, the fading patter of raindrops on the forest leaves.

'I've got to get him,' said the Kid softly, 'Or he'll get me.'

CHAPTER XIX

The Column

Drawing his long bowie-knife, the Kid started his stalk for the point where he had seen Spotted Fawn. He counted the yards, and then froze, waiting for a sound or sight that would again betray his enemy to him.

There came a faint flash of lightning. Spotted Fawn was no longer at the slide, was not visible to Bob Pryor.

With an inward curse, unable to guess which way his foe had gone, the Kid slid for the drop into the gulch. He had to get across. Without bumping into the Sioux, he reached the descent, and began feeling his way down, sharp rocks cutting his soaked body.

He came to the stream, waded in, splashing over to the other side and pulling up into the rocks. To his right was that narrow opening, yet he was sure the Sioux would have it covered, so turned the other way instead. He felt his way along, then cursed to himself as his moccasin-covered foot rattled one stone against another.

Something moved just ahead, and he froze, knife in his strong bronzed hand, peering ahead into the misty gloom. A second later, by a flash in the sky, he saw Spotted Fawn right

164

before him, a revolver drawn. And, huddled against a granite cliff wall, staring across the gulch, was the thin form of Celestino Mireles. The hawk-like face of the Mexican was anxious, drawn, as his eyes sought the woods above, where stood the stockade.

Spotted Fawn had glimpsed Mireles, the faithful lad seeking to find what fate had come upon his General, the Rio Kid, and those he desired to save from death. Now the Sioux, with his cruel lips drawn in a taut line, cocked his gun to kill the Mex. But, seizing that moment of light the Kid launched himself through the air.

The gun banged, flashed in the night. But already Pryor had landed on Spotted Fawn's back, bearing him to the rocks. Again the Indian's pistol roared, the burning powder and slug singeing the Kid's ear.

'Damn yore red hide!' growled the Kid, his knife driving deep and straight for the heart, under the shoulder blade.

The Sioux fought like a panther and his greased body was difficult to hold. He was trying to get his pistol around to blow the Kid's belly out. But the Kid had seized Spotted Fawn's wrist, twisting the muzzle away, just as for a third time the pistol exploded with Spotted Fawn's finger on the trigger.

The Kid twisted the handle of the long-bladed bowie. Spotted Fawn was still writhing in his grip. Then the powerful Indian suddenly ceased to fight as the knife point found his heart. Spotted Fawn shuddered, went limp in the powerful hold of the Rio Kid.

Ripping out the knife, the Kid leaped to his feet. The shots that had banged through the canyon would no doubt be heard by the keen ears of other warriors.

'Celestino!' he called softly.

'General—I am here!'

Due to the Rio Kid's quick work, Spotted Fawn's first slug had spattered the rocks at the Mexican's feet, instead of killing him.

Joyfully Mireles came to the Rio Kid's side, gripped his hand.

'I look for you, General! Ees hard, to wait so, *si*.'

'C'mon, we gotta light outa here! There's a thousand Sioux in them woods!'

'All through the gulch, too, General! I hav' hard time to come so close!'

'Is there a way up near? How'd yuh come down?'

'I show you,' said the Mexican.

Mireles seized the Kid's hand and guided him rapidly north for a hundred yards to where a lone pine tree had sprouted in the dirt. Up its bare, resin-sticky limbs, spaced like a ladder, the Mexican led the Rio Kid.

The storm was about over. Thunder rumbled grumpily in the distance, and the lightning had finished its startling display. In pitch blackness, with the drip-drip of the water from the leaves and needles of the conifers, the only sound, the two stepped out on the east rim of Deadwood Gulch and streaked for the woods up the slope.

'Yuh see that gang of fake Injuns?' growled the Kid, gasping for breath after the run, as they reached the cover of the forest.

'*Si*, General. Zey go east, before ze Sioux comes thees mornin'.'

'Huh. Keepin' outa the way, I reckon. I'll lay a thousand to a bit that that gang had Spotted Fawn sic the Sioux on us!'

'Where yuh go now, General?'

'Goin' to fetch help, Celestino.'

Mireles took him through the forest aisles, snaking through the dense bush. Saber scented his master, and sniffed with joy, nuzzling the Kid's wet hand.

The Kid slapped saddle on the dun, who perked up at signs of action.

'I have hard time to hol' heem when he hear ze battle, General,' said Mireles. 'He weesh to fight.'

'Uh, huh.' The Kid was ready to ride.

'Wait! I go weesh you.'

'All right. But yuh'll hafta ride fast, boy.'

'How you hope to fin' help in ze heels?'

'Depends how near Custer is. It's a toss-up. Also how long that stockade holds out.'

The pine woods were black. They talked in low whispers, as they swung east out of the concealing thickets. A forlorn hope, but the only one for the whites trapped in the stockade on the opposite hill.

Cracklings came from behind them. That might be made by animals, or by Sioux scouts who had been alarmed by the shots in the gulch where Spotted Fawn's carcass was buzzard-bait.

The storm which had made it possible for the Kid to creep through the Sioux lines was entirely past now. The clouds were speeding across the sky, and the stars gave the Kid his direction.

Eastward he shoved the dun, letting the horse's instinct pick a way through. Hour after hour the steady pace of the long-legged Saber ate up the miles from Deadwood, while the Rio Kid traveled on alone, for on this vital mission he had left his young Mexican friend behind.

'Custer, Custer,' he muttered, as the first light of the new day grayed the heavens, 'how far are yuh?'

Back there, huddled in the stockade, were his friends—Billy North, Billy's dying sweetheart, Wild Bill and Calamity, the folks Burton had led into the Black Hills. They were buoyed only by the slight hope that the Kid might get through, might find some way to bring help to them.

He was riding a deer trail, along a high ridge when the sun touched the sky with a rosy hue, overwhelming the grayness. The dun suddenly threw up his head, snorted and pressed eagerly forward, picking up speed.

'What is it, Saber? What yuh hear that I didn't?'

The keen animal senses could outmatch man's, even such highly trained senses as those of the Rio Kid.

But Pryor could not make out anything, and for another mile he shoved along. The wind of speed had dried his clothing that was torn and covered with muck from his crawling in the night. His face was powderstained, streaks of bronzed skin showed where sweat had made furrows, and dried blood runnels from his clotted ear wound were on one cheek.

Again the dun sniffed, quivered, and this time the Kid shouted aloud with joy.

'I hear it, now!' he cried. 'Reveille! Army bugles! Yuh're right, Saber!'

Those clear calls were distant, but not so distant that he could not reach them shortly. Hastily he bore off in the direction of the sounds ...

The sun had lost its early morning roseate hue when the lathered dun, carrying the bedraggled Rio Kid, swung down a pine-covered slope and headed for the van of the long army column.

Strung for a mile in the wide valley through which they were traveling came the blue army columns. They traveled slowly, accommodating their pace to the heaving teams of draught horses and mules that drew the blue-painted, canvas-topped supply wagons, and to the herd of beef cattle plodding in the rear-meat for the troops.

Wheels sank deep in virgin earth, for Custer was making his first official survey of the great wilderness, exploring the Hills. The expedition traveled in four columns, in protected position, cavalry lines riding the flanks, Ree and Crow scouts out ahead and checking the rear guard.

The sun rays glinted from burnished accoutrements, from sabers and carbines. Blue uniforms were spick and span, felt hats curved at regulation angle. With guidons flying, the ten companies of cavalry formed the bulk of the troops with General Custer, although two companies of infantry also were with the expedition, as well as scientists assigned to check the unknown riches of the Black Hills.

In the distance, the cathedral spires topping the bare crest of Harvey's Peak could be seen, while the curling grass was literally carpeted with gaily hued wild flowers. Bold, lofty summits of lesser peaks loomed up, clad in black pines, granite abutments reaching toward the sky.

But the Rio Kid, forging ahead to get help for his hard-pressed friends in the Deadwood stockade, saw only those slowly creeping blue columns.

A bugle rang, then another. He was about a mile from the van of the United States forces when an Indian, swinging around a wooded bend, suddenly saw him coming and threw up his carbine, uttering a hoarse shout.

'Hey Long Back! Don't shoot! It's the Kid!'

Long Back recognized his voice, then recognized the dun. As Pryor rode up, the Indian stared in amazement at the once trim figure of the Rio Kid.

'Huh!' he grunted. 'You drag self through mudhole. Where you go, huh?'

'Is Pahuska comin', Long Back? The Sioux are half a sun's ride west, attackin' some whites.'

'Sure, him hunt up front,' replied the Ree.

His dark nostrils dilated at mention of the Sioux, his hereditary enemy—the Sioux who in their proud might had conquered lesser tribes, the Crows and Rees, decimating them, and swarming over their tribal lands. Conquerors in their own right, the Sioux now were faced by a race of another color, too numerous to be wiped out, or beaten back; an ever pressing tidal wave, deadly for the red man.

There were more scouts, Crows and Rees, in the bush on the ridges, checking the advance of Custer's columns. They noted the Rio Kid as he spoke with Long Back, and recognized the rangy dun as Pryor rode toward the van of the army forces.

Custer was always to be found up front. He liked to ride out of sight of his troopers with a few favorite officers, hunting, observing the natural sights of the country he was crossing. A couple of huge, shaggy hounds—Custer's dogs—dashed past the Kid baying. Pahuska, George Custer, came driving full tilt after his dogs. The tall, handsome Custer rode like a centaur, on Dandy, one of his favorite mounts. He wore fringed bucksin, black boots with army spurs, and a wide Stetson that shaded his handsome, masterful face.

Behind him rode a group of officers, and several civilian members of the scientific expedition into the Black Hills. They were biologists and mining engineers, come to collect data in the virgin wilderness.

Among the group of officers the Kid recognized Tom Custer, a U.S. Army captain, George's younger brother. He was a large man with the mischievous, glowing health of youth.

Custer caught sight of the Kid bearing toward him on the lathered dun. He reined in short, staring. His yellowish mustache bristled as he dropped a hand quickly to one of his pistols.

'General!' cried the Kid. 'It's Bob Pryor!'

Custer spurred toward him, his forehead wrinkled to a frown.

'How in blazes did you get here?' demanded Custer, astounded. 'Winters said you'd headed for the Missouri!'

'I ain't got time to talk now, General Custer,' the Rio Kid said earnestly. 'I'll answer all charges against me, but right now there's a bunch of white men and women besieged in a stockade over in Deadwood Gulch. There's a thousand Sioux warriors under Gall and Sittin' Bull ringin' 'em. It depends how fast yuh get there whether they live or die.'

Custer's eyes flashed with quick anger. The Kid knew the general's temper, and held his breath, hoping this was not to be an explosion against himself. That accusation of having murdered a soldier was a serious one.

'Whites are not permitted in the Black Hills!' Custer said harshly. 'They've only themselves to thank for this.'

But he was already signaling a staff officer.

'Captain Davis! The Gray Horse Troop and the White Horse Troop, immediately! Make sure they have emergency ammunition. Tom, come here!'

CHAPTER XX

Defeat

Rapidly the general gave his instructions as his brother rode over and waited for commands. Captain Davis was already spurring back to fetch the advance guard ordered by Custer. A guard of infantry and two troops of cavalry would remain with the expedition while Tom Custer would follow up the general and his van with the rest of the mounted troops.

'Fetch a surgeon, suh,' begged the Kid. 'There's a young white woman wounded in that stockade and she needs expert care quick as she can get it! Others 're hurt, too.'

Custer nodded. He finished giving his orders, and swung to speak again with his former aide-de-camp, Bob Pryor.

'I'm ready to answer to that murder charge, General,' Pryor told his old commander earnestly, 'soon as this is cleared up. I'd like to guide yuh to that Deadwood Gulch and make shore them folks are saved.'

To his surprise and relief, George Custer growled:

'What charge are yuh talking about?'

'Why, you know,' explained the Kid, searching the stern eyes of the great cavalry leader. 'The one yuh sent to Cap'n Winters to arrest me for the stabbin' of a soldier near the Fort.'

'Stuff and nonsense!' snapped Custer. 'I never believed that cock-and-bull story, Pryor. It's true that your knife was used to kill that trooper, but Charlie Reynolds cleared that up. He told me you'd been with him all evening, and that he knew you'd lost your knife at Sitting Bull's camp before the killing. We decided one of the Sioux had done the job.'

'Huh! Jest the same, I'd like to get to the bottom of it . . . Did yuh savvy that a written order, signed by you, was delivered to Cap'n Winters to arrest me? It throwed me off, and that's how come Winters' advance guard got hit so bad!'

'I understand. I had a written report from Winters, telling me he had destroyed Cherryville, and mentioning the fact that you'd "got away." I expected to clear that statement up when Winters joined us. He's due to connect with us before long.'

'Is Lieutenant Spanghorn here, suh?'

Custer nodded. It was Spanghorn, the arresting troopers had said, who had transmitted the written order for his arrest.

'He's at the rear, in charge of the commissary,' Custer said.

There was no time to thrash out puzzles now, though. Already Captain Davis was swinging into view at the head of the Gray Horse and White Horse troops, Custer's crack cavalry, each troop mounted on horses of the same approximate color and size. Their Spencer carbines were at regulation angle. Their blue uniform pants, with wide yellow cavalry stripes on the seams, were tucked into shining boots. Blue tunics were smartly fastened, and wide-brimmed Stetsons set at jaunty angles.

Officers and non-coms rode the flanks, and the short-flagged guidons waved in the breeze.

In perfect formation they approached their commander, George A. Custer.

The general swung into position at the head of his forces, and snapped an order. Bugles blew the advance, they headed west and north for Deadwood, guided by the Rio Kid who kept his dun out front.

'I shore hope they hold out till we get there,' muttered the Kid.

The trip back took longer than the run the Rio Kid had made as he had ridden in search of Custer's columns. On the way they met Mireles, following in his partner's trail. The Kid gave the young Mexican some quick instructions, and Celestino rode south while the soldiers kept on toward Deadwood.

It was still light when Custer and the Kid, with troopers riding lathered horses behind, broke over the crest through the woods. They scanned the woods across the gulch, and the stockade above in the rocks.

'There're the Sioux, General!' cried the Kid.

A rifle crackled from the west. Savage eyes had spied the soldiers approaching. The Kid heard the threatening shriek of the bullet over their heads.

'Remington, and the newest make at that,' exclaimed Custer bitterly. 'Some day I'll scotch that Indian Bureau, Pryor. They exploit the Indians, steal their moneys, and trade them our first-grade war materials for their furs and riches. Then cheat them, then egg them on to fight the Army.'

A command rang out, and the troopers dismounted, seizing their Spencers and ammunition pouches crammed with shells. Bullets were dropping from the high woods across the canyon, spitting into the pines and leaves, kicking up dirt. The soldiers showed no excitement, coolly forming under their general's orders.

The terrain made it impossible to ride across to engage the Sioux. Custer meant to charge them afoot.

Barbaric figures showed in great numbers in the woods, as chiefs and sub-chiefs sprang up to view the soldiers. The late afternoon sun gleamed on Pahuska's long yellow hair, a scalp coveted by many a Sioux. It was not sporting to wear short hair when on Indian campaigns, for the savages considered it a sign of weakness. Long hair meant that a man was ready to vaunt his scalp and protect it.

'Spread out, boys,' Custer ordered.

His voice, though stern, had a pleased ring to it. Battle was his meat and drink. Danger meant everything to George Armstrong Custer.

'Captain, put a few shots into those woods,' he ordered. 'But be careful not to hit the stockade.'

A bugle blew the charge. The Spencers began whipping slugs at the Sioux. The van started down the slope toward Deadwood Gulch, led by the Rio Kid and General Custer. For a brief instant, the Kid glimpsed Sitting Bull and Chief Gall, watching the soldiers advance.

Gun in hand, ready to drive the savages from their prey, the Kid hit the rim of the gulch first of all. Custer ran up, squatted beside him. Bullets were ricocheting off the rocks, spattering them with fragments of lead and stone, as the general's practiced eye took in the rough terrain, estimating the numbers of the foe.

'How many did you say, Pryor?' he asked.

'A thousand warriors. Mebbe more.'

'I won't put the advance guard through that gulch and up that bare stretch of slope,' Custer declared. 'Not without support.'

Lined along the east rim of the canyon, his troopers waited for orders.

More bugles blew from the rear. The Kid looked back over his shoulder, and saw Tom Custer break from the woods, in the van of the main body of cavalry. And at the same moment, the Sioux, starting down to engage the two troops with Custer, caught sight of the main body of troops coming in.

Custer signaled, called an order to his adjutant. Bugles blew in the gulch. Dismounted, the troopers, with Spencers ready and loaded, hurried to the brink. Custer's main body was up.

A burst of gunfire shrieked from Sioux guns, then the general sprang up, the Kid with him. Ways were found down into the canyon, and the crossing began, the thin lines crawling up the other side. Custer and Pryor were first on the west side. The general, saber in hand, stood coolly erect as bullets sang about his long-maned head.

'Charge!' shrilled the bugles.

'There they go, General!' shouted the Kid, and the two ran up the slope after the Sioux.

The Indians were melting away to the west, over the hills, through the woods. Down below where their hairy mustangs were waiting, they were springing on their horses, riding rapidly away from Deadwood.

The kid swung up to the crest of rocks. The battered stockade was before them. From it came hoarse cheers. The Kid, pressing eagerly in, saw a hat, perforated by bullet holes, sail into the air. Then the gate opened and Wild Bill Hickok, with Calamity Jane at his side, leaped forward to grasp the Kid's hand.

'Yuh made it, dawggone yore hide!' cried Wild Bill.

Custer's long legs took him to the stockade and he strode through the gate. His troopers had halted as the Sioux retreated westward.

Wounded, gaunt and exhausted survivors lay about the stockade. But some were able to stand erect and greet their saviors.

'Howdy, General,' drawled Wild Bill.

179

'Hickok!' exclaimed Custer.

At Hays City, Wild Bill had had a run in with three of the general's troopers, and had fled Custer's wrath, but this little misunderstanding had been smoothed over. Hickok had scouted for Custer in earlier days.

Billy North, face grim and drawn, stepped eagerly forward. 'How about the surgeon?' he croaked. 'She's mighty near gone.'

An army doctor, kit in hand, pressed forward. He hurried to the silent, pale-faced girl who was sheltered by a piece of tarpaulin and covered with blankets. He knelt beside her.

'Heat water,' the Kid heard him say, after his examination of Edith.

'They pot-shotted at us all day, Kid,' Calamity Jane Canary informed Pryor, who sank down to rest. 'We was dang near outa ammunition. Lucky they didn't attack agin. Yuh're shore a welcome sight.'

The first concern was care of the battered whites in the stockade. Food and warm drinks, were ordered by Custer, wounds were attended to, and slight injuries bound by willing troopers. The more serious awaited attention by the surgeon, busy with Edith Burton.

The doctor was making ready to operate, to extract the murderous lead slug that prevented the girl from rallying. 'Who's in charge here?' Custer demanded.

Uncle Dan Olliphant, a bullet singe on one apple-red cheek, and his left arm in a sling, stepped forward, smiling.

'Reckon I am, now that Jake Burton's dead, General!'

'You see now, sir, what a foolhardy thing you've done in entering the Black Hills,' Custer said severely. 'While I can't allow the Indians to kill United States citizens, the government has issued strict instructions that all whites arrested here be ejected, by force if necessary, and their supplies and wagons confiscated. As soon as your people can move you'll be escorted to the edge of the reservation.'

'Yes, suh, General,' agreed Uncle Dan wearily.

They had paid a fearful price for the Sioux gold, and now they were to lose all claim to the yellow metal which had lured them.

Night was upon them. Custer's pickets were out, his troopers camped in the woods below the stockade with fires burning. The tired folks of Deadwood slept.

The Kid, too, could relax at last. He was aware, as he dropped off, that the surgeon was watching Edith Burton carefully, and would remain at the girl's side through the night . . .

Pryor awoke in the fresh dawn. People were stirring about him, and he heard the clear notes of the bugle sounding reveille, and, shortly after, mess call. General Custer, in fresh buckskin, was having his breakfast among his field officers, in a clearing below the stockade. The aromatic odor of coffee and frying meat, reached the Kid's nostrils. He sniffed hungrily.

Billy North stepped over, and the young hunter was smiling. He gripped the Kid's hand.

'She's better!' Pryor exclaimed.

'Shore is! The doc says she'll get well, Kid! I never felt so happy afore. Nothin' makes any difference beside her. Yuh saved her and all of us.'

Pryor turned away, washed up and cleaned himself so far as possible, then strolled down toward the soldiers.

Custer signaled him, and the Kid went over.

'Sit down and have some breakfast with us, Pryor,' invited the general. He turned back to the surgeon. 'How long until that girl can safely be moved, Doctor?'

'Oh, a week,' the surgeon replied. 'Then she'll need an ambulance. The rest seem all right. They need rest and attention, that's all.'

Custer made his decision.

'I'll leave a guard here, to escort them out when the time comes, and return to the main camp.'

The Rio Kid, squatted near his old commander, ate a hearty meal, strength flowing fresh into his lithe body. He kept silent, watching the officers. Now that he had

182

time to think, he was turning over in his mind all that he had uncovered on his mission to the Black Hills, begun when Custer had sent Charlie Reynolds and himself to trace a leak in missing army supplies.

'There's still half of Kansas Joe's gang hidin' out in the Hills, ready to grab everything in sight,' he thought. 'And though Murphy's dead and Spotted Fawn is buzzard bait, they've still got their Chief.'

'And when Custer marches on, the Chief will have a free hand in the Hills.'

The Kid went over to his saddle which was hanging with the rest of his rig on a tree limb. He had left Saber free to forage during the night. Reaching in a saddle-bag, he extracted the gold tunic button he had picked up, back on the trail to Fort Lincoln, the button left by that skulking dry-gulcher.

'When I find the man who lost this,' he mused, 'I'll be steppin' in the right direction!'

There were plenty of army officers around —lieutenants, a couple of captains, a major. The Kid observed them all, then shook his head.

'Need more, I reckon,' he decided.

CHAPTER XXI

A Brass Button

Soon after breakfast, Bob Pryor saddled up the dun and rode back east with Custer, who, having left all but his Gray Horse Troop disposed about Deadwood, was returning to his main camp.

In the late afternoon they sighted the tents and canvas-topped wagons of Custer's exploring party. The camp was in trim military order, everything and everyone in place. Civilian scientists were out, busily engaged in collecting specimens of minerals, bugs and wild flowers.

Bob Pryor left Saber at the horse lines, where the dun proceeded to make himself king of the mountain by bullying the army plugs. The Kid strolled toward Officers' Row. Trim, neatly uniformed army men of Custer's staff were about, and the Kid's blue eyes quickly looked them over.

Captain Frank Winters, in a clean uniform, and others he had encountered during his work for Custer, were there. Custer was a stickler for discipline, and insisted on his subordinates living up to army tradition.

As the lithe Kid strolled toward the scouts, Celestino Mireles came hurrying toward him.

The slim Mexican smiled as he greeted his own general.

'Are they at the box canyon?' the Kid inquired quickly.

'*Si*, General! Soupy Greegs ees weeth zem, and pairhaps feefty men. Zey hide zere, at ze place where I rescue yuh zat night.'

'Huh! Custer'll be interested. Them army stores he's been huntin' are cached there. But we'll have to hit fast, 'fore they find that I've escaped that Sioux massacre the Chief planned! I don't doubt he sicked Sitting Bull on Deadwood, damn his hide!'

'Here comes Charlie Reynolds,' Mireles observed. 'Long ride, from ze east.'

The Kid swung and saw his friend, the great scout, ride in on a lathered mustang. Reynolds had a three-days' beard growth, his clothing was spattered with dried mud and torn from clutching thorns and bush during his obviously long ride.

He dismounted and, stiff from hours in the saddle, approached Custer's headquarters.

The Kid hustled up.

'Howdy, Charlie! Where yuh hail from?'

'Been on a secret trip for the General, Kid,' answered Lonesome Charlie in a low, husky voice. 'I'm carryin' special dispatches for Custer. Tell yuh more later, after I've reported.'

Reynolds nodded and, passed by Custer's order to the sentries, disappeared inside the big tent.

The Rio Kid had plenty to turn over in his clever mind as he walked slowly down Officers' Row, nodding to friends. Tom Custer, having changed his uniform after the run over to Deadwood, emerged from his quarters and paused to chat with the Kid, whom he had known for years.

'Good afternoon, Major,' Tom Custer said, glancing past Pryor. 'Have a good trip, sir?'

Major Hanson Clyde, every detail of his tall, precise figure correct, smiled and nodded.

'Yes thank you, Captain. I'm on my way now to report to the general. How's his health?'

'Fine, fine. When did you get back?'

'After noon.'

Hanson Clyde passed on toward Custer's tent.

'Where's he been?' asked the Kid.

'The general sent him to the Missouri, on a special mission,' replied Tom Custer. Lowering his voice he added: 'I know I can trust you, Pryor, for you've been working on the same thing. It had to do with the diversion of military supplies in this district.'

'I savvy.'

After a few minutes Reynolds emerged, and Major Clyde went in to report to General Custer. The Kid left Captain Tom and joined Reynolds.

'C'mon, Kid,' Lonesome Charlie said to

Pryor. 'I got a lot to tell yuh. But I'm starvin'. I'm goin' to see if I can beg a meal from the cook.'

The teeming, busy camp life went on about them. Reynolds obtained some cold meat and bread and drink, and while wolfing the viands he talked to the Rio Kid, between bites.

'Kid, I toted Custer's report to the government that gold has been discovered on French Crik,' confided Reynolds. 'I rode to Yankton, and picked up telegraphed dispatches from Washington. The big thing is this: President Grant's openin' the Black Hills to white settlement, on account of the many killin's and friction between whites and the Sioux in here, and pressure 'cause of the discovery of gold.'

'That means war, sure as hell!' growled the Kid. 'Sittin' Bull'll never take it lyin' down. Custer don't like it, either.'

'Huh! No doubt. But Custer'll have to obey his orders. He's a soldier first of all. If yuh look far ahead, Kid, yuh'll see the U. S. can't leave a big stumblin' block like Dakota that splits the Nation in two. It's tough on the Indians, but they'll have to go onto reservations as Government wards.'

Pryor nodded. Lonesome Charlie's somber eyes sought the majestic sweep of the Black Hills where Harney's Peak, its serrated crest flanked by feathery white clouds, towered over the land.

'At Custer's order, I checked up with the military commandant at Yankton,' went on Reynolds. 'The information you and me picked up for Custer riled him powerful, and he sent me secret-like over to the depot there. I fetched him back a bunch of requisition orders, and Custer claims they're forged!'

'I savvy! That's how them supplies that was marked condemned got into Kansas Joe's hands! Charlie, Joe's dead and so's Spotted Fawn and half that gang. The rest of 'em are still on the loose, Soupy Griggs among 'em. And the most dangerous of all, the hombre I figger thought all this up, is free. He's after Deadwood and I reckon he'll get it if he ain't stopped!'

Mess call blew, and the soldiers and civilian members of the expedition went to eat. But the Kid waited a moment and sidetracked General Custer as he emerged from his quarters.

'General,' he told him, so that only Custer heard, 'I reckon I can lead yuh to some of them stolen supplies. They're cached in a box canyon not many miles south of here.'

'Good! We'll go after them in the morning.'

Custer was visibly affected by the news Reynolds had brought from Yankton, on the Missouri. The opening of the Black Hills to whites meant war, and he knew it. And the general was aware that there was a traitor in his ranks.

The Kid ate with the other scouts. Dark fell, and bivouac fires glowed yellow in the night.

Continuing his quiet hunt for the insidious, hidden Chief, who had through his machinations and desire for gold caused the death of so many innocents and hurried the confiscation of the Black Hills by the government, Pryor strolled along the row of officer tents.

Then his keen nostrils caught an aromatic odor that brought him up short. He swung, saw an officer sitting on a box at his tent door.

'Howdy, Lieutenant Spanghorn,' he drawled. 'Yore cigar smells mighty good.'

'Sorry I can't offer you one,' Spanghorn said politely. 'It's a special west Indian cheroot, Pryor.'

'Could I have a word with yuh, private-like?' asked the Kid.

'Certainly. Come inside.'

The large, dark-haired, taciturn officer turned toward his tent, his broad shoulders, in his blue tunic hunched.

An hour later, the Rio Kid quietly approached a darkened tent. The coast seemed clear. He slipped through the flap and stood in the dark little cubicle for a moment, orienting his eyes. Red light against the canvas sides, from the fires, gave enough illumination for him to make out large objects although he could not distinguish details.

After a few moments, he found a mud-spattered, torn tunic, cast in a corner under a blanket. Eagerly he took from his pocket the brass button, with a small piece of ragged cloth still clinging to it, for the dirtied coat he held had a button missing from the front, a tiny rip where the metal had pulled out a bit of the material.

To make absolutely certain, excited by the terrible evidence he had uncovered, the Kid struck a match, shading it with his body and hand. The tiny pattern attached to the button fitted exactly into the hole in the tunic.

'I got him!' he muttered. 'The Chief!'

Suddenly he dropped the match, whirling. A gun banged from the flap entry, and the Kid was knocked flat on his face as blackness swirled down upon him.

Instantly a hullabaloo rose in the army camp. Armed guards rushed toward the scene as General Custer dashed forth, pistol up. A shadowy figure slunk swiftly away from the tent where the still figure of the Rio Kid lay crumpled in the dirt . . .

When the Rio Kid came to, his head ached frightfully. It felt tremendously swollen as gingerly he put a hand up, feeling the wadded bandage placed on his scalp crease by an army doctor.

A soldier nurse was supposed to be caring for him, but there was a hubbub outside, and the sun was yellow in the sky. The trooper was outside, staring down the camp.

The Kid pushed himself up, licking dry lips. He reached for a canteen nearby, took a drink. He found he could rise, and though shaky on his legs, he stepped forth into the fresh new day.

'Musta been out all night,' he muttered.

The nurse swung, and cursed. 'Say, you're s'posed to be in bed,' he objected.

'Well, I ain't. What's all the fuss about?'

'They say Sittin' Bull's comin'!'

The Kid pushed past the soldier, and staggered down the company street.

Sitting Bull, on a beautiful pink-and-white paint mustang, came riding majestically, alone, into the camp of Custer. The medicine man of the Sioux was fierce as any jungle beast, with the cunning of a fine, scheming brain behind his power. The solid, stocky body sat the blanketed back of the paint horse as though part of the beast, a red centaur.

Arms folded, Sitting Bull was trailed by scouts and soldiers who had brought him through at Custer's command. His face, high-boned, with eagle beak and sinister eyes, were forbidding as he drew up before General George A. Custer. Custer greeted the great medicine man kindly, but Sitting Bull gave no sign of friendship.

'Yellow Hair,' the Indian said, 'the word has come to the Sioux that the Great White Father has taken the Black Hills from the

Indians. The bones of the buffalo herds are bleaching on the plains and the Indian must now become a beggar, living on what scraps the white man tosses him. Our hunting grounds are destroyed, our sacred land stolen. The Sioux must be crowded onto reservations where they are fed like captive beasts on rotten meat. But I, Sitting Bull, will never consent to this nor will the bravest of my people. There will be war, Pahuska.'

'Sitting Bull,' replied Custer, 'I am a soldier. I must obey the orders that are given to me. I have sought to help the Sioux, to keep the peace and see justice done to the Indian. But you know that if there is war, then I will fight for my people.'

'You are a good fighter, a warrior, Pahuska. The Sioux know that and for that they like you. We hate cowards. Therefore we will never hate ourselves. Prepare for war, Yellow Hair!'

CHAPTER XXII

The White Chief Pays

Viciously the Sioux chief and medicine man jerked his reins, swinging the handsome paint horse. He kicked his heels against the creamy ribs of the stallion and sped away from the camp.

As the men in camp watched and listened, a defiant, shrill war-whoop rang from Sitting Bull's throat.

Custer stared grimly after the dwindling figure of the medicine man.

'General,' thc Kid said softly, sliding up beside him, 'I got information that can't wait.'

Custer turned, frowning, startled from a reverie of what was to come.

'What is it, Pryor?'

The Kid spoke swiftly, his voice so low that only his old commander of Civil War days could hear.

'I reckon I can identify the head of the trouble that come on the Hills, suh. I talked with Lieutenant Spanghorn, who told me the name of the officer on yore staff who give him that forged order for my arrest. No doubt Reynolds brought yuh more of the same, that diverted yore military supplies to Cherryville, Murphy's camp.

'I whiffed a queer-smellin' tobacco smoke several times, even picked up a black cheroot butt, General, that this here Chief, as his outlaws call him, fancies. Spanghorn was smokin' one of 'em. He told me who gave it to him, and a brass button I picked up on the trail where this Chief had been fits the tunic of this same hombre. Yuh got a traitor, an important traitor, on yore staff, suh.'

'I know that,' Custer replied. 'I'm on his

trail, Pryor. You were creased last night. What were you doing in that tent?'

'Checkin' on the man yuh want, General. He smokes them fancy West Indian cheroots, and it was his tunic that had the button gone from it! He's the head of this whole dirty business that's hustled the Sioux from the Hills. He never went to Yankton as yuh thought. Instead, he rode down here, tried to drygulch me on the way. He's had charge of the outlaw gang, and he planned the game, his object bein' to take control of Deadwood Gulch and get possession when the Hills were throwed open to settlement. This had to happen, sooner or later, with the killin's and friction he caused.'

'His name?' demanded Custer.

'Major Hanson Clyde!'

Custer swore under his breath, swinging on his spurred heel. He snapped an order to Tom Custer, near at hand, and Tom hurried away. After a time he returned.

'Clyde's not in camp, Autie,' the Kid heard Tom report to his famous brother, using the family nickname. 'A sentry says he left before dawn.'

'We better get after him, General,' the Kid suggested. 'A man like that can cause a hell of a lot of trouble!'

Custer quickly gave his commands. Bugles blew, and troopers hurried to saddle up and fall into line . . .

A few hours later the Rio Kid, out ahead of cavalry, on his swift dun, saw before him the bush-fringed entrance to the box canyon. He slid from Saber's back, and crept forward.

Flat on his belly, he whiffed a faint odor of frying beef that drifted on the warm air out of the narrow opening. Then he heard the low whinny of a mustang and knew that men were hidden in there.

'It's Clyde I got to have,' he muttered. 'Damn his hide!'

He returned to the dun, and sped back the way he had come, to hurry up the troopers under Captain Tom Custer's command.

Inside of an hour he led them to the box canyon. The Kid, Colt in hand and bending low over Saber, was first to spur through into the hide-out.

Up the canyon he saw Soupy Lou Griggs, surrounded by fifty of Murphy's outlaws. They were lounging about, drinking, unaware of danger.

At sight of the Kid, Soupy leaped to his feet, screaming the alarm.

Fierce-faced bandits reached for pistols and rifles. The Kid put a shot between Soupy Griggs' feet, and Lou Griggs fell down, crying for mercy.

Tom Custer, with saber drawn, urged his troopers to follow as he came charging in the Rio Kid's wake. Bullets sang past Pryor's head, and he fired, his smashing lead ripping

195

into the milling killers, some of them still in their Sioux disguise.

The soldiers came crowding in. They leaped from their horses, snatching loaded carbines, and running at the foe. For a few moments bullets flew back and forth, oaths rang with the gunshots in the box canyon. The Kid, driving Saber around the flank of the enemy, shoved into the rocks against the wall. He picked off the outlaw lieutenants who whipped their men to fight.

The troopers' rifles snapped, a volley that tore into the ranks of the bandits. Half a dozen of them fell. 'Stop it!' Soupy Griggs was yelling. 'Don't shoot! We quit!'

The bandits could not stand the charge of the seasoned fighting men. Guns stopped roaring, were thrown down as hands rose in surrender.

The Kid shoved the dun up, leaped down, grabbed Soupy Griggs by the neck, and stood the shaking rat upright. 'We're onto yore game, Griggs,' he snarled. 'Where's Clyde, yore Chief!'

'He ain't here, so help me!' quavered Soupy. 'He ain't been here since we got back from Deadwood!'

He was willing to talk, for he feared the Kid from the bottom of his craven soul.

He pointed out the hiding places of the military stores, diverted by Major Hanson Clyde, a trusted member of Custer's staff, and answered all the questions snapped at him by Bob Pryor.

'Clyde didn't come over here last night,' the Kid told Tom Custer. 'I reckon I savvy what he's up to. He knowed the jig was up, and didn't try to save Griggs' gang. I'll leave the prisoners and these supplies to yuh, and I'll be ridin'.'

'Where you going, Kid?' asked Tom Custer.

'On Clyde's trail. *Adios.*'

With Celestino Mireles, the Rio Kid from the box canyon . . .

After long weary hours of riding, the Rio Kid spurred the dun out of the shady, inviting mountains southeast, into the Bad Lands adjoining the Black Hills. Dust and runnels of sweat covered the powerful horse, and the Kid had a grim look to his narrowed eyes that were fixed on the sign of the horseman before him.

By clever figuring and trailing he had come out right, and had picked up Major Hanson Clyde's sign.

The sun-drenched, water-gashed land across which he was riding, carved out by winds and rains of centuries from a prehistoric ocean of soft rock and mud, stuck up myriad fantastic shapes. Great turrets and castles, terraces, walls and cities.

Strange-colored buttes in pastel shades of pink, red, blue, black, green and contrasting hues surrounded the Kid as he wove on that trail of the arch-murderer whose cunning had come so near to finishing his career, and who might even now be still uncovered had it not been for Bob Pryor's clever work.

Then the Rio Kid, topping a crumbling rock rise stained rusty from mineral content, saw his man ahead, crossing a desertlike stretch on a limping black horse.

'Luck's with me,' thought the Kid. 'I thought that hoss of his was slowin' down!'

He spurred ahead, Colts ready in their oiled holsters at his hips.

Clyde swung in his leather, catching the steady beat of the dun's hoofs coming up on him. His massive head of curling black hair was crowned by an army Stetson, and he still wore the fresh uniform to which he had changed at Custer's camp.

'Halt, Major!' bawled the Kid. 'Yuh're under arrest! General Custer's orders!'

As Pryor rapidly gained, he could see the man's furious face, the set, wide mouth, the jut of the chin. Clyde's dark eyes flashed a red warning to the Rio Kid, and the traitor dropped his hand to his Colt, whipped out his weapon and fired.

The slug whistled within an inch of the Kid's low-bent head as he galloped the dun hell-for-leather, straight at his foe, the man on whose trail he had stuck for so long. Pryor swung up his pistol, as Clyde, steadying his black, sought for a death aim.

The major's gun again spat fire and lead. But it was already dropping, for the Rio Kid had let go. Clyde's second one hit the sand ahead of Bob Pryor, as the Kid, Colt up, pulled to a sliding stop.

Hanson Clyde collapsed in his leather, his big body folding up. The dun bit at the black, who shied.

A bullet hole showed between Clyde's widened, staring eyes as he was jerked loose from saddle. He fell in a heap on the hot earth.

A shout from the ridge behind told the Kid that Mireles was coming up. He bent over Clyde, and saw the bulge in the dead traitor's tunic.

Celestino, lashing his tired mustang, drew up beside the Rio Kid.

Pryor was squatted beside the dead man. He had spread out a large paper, while others, taken from inside the slain Clyde's tunic, rested in a pile close at hand.

'Look at this, Celestino,' growled the Rio Kid. 'A map of the Black Hills, Clyde's work! He was Custer's army engineer. Here's Deadwood and dozens of other spots marked.' He shuffled through the other papers. 'Claims, minin' claims to the best placers in the Hills, ready for filin'. And see, there's other valuable stuff he spotted. Look! Rock oil that's this new petroleum stuff they're startin' to make such a fuss about —iron and cobalt . . . Why, the rascal would have been an emperor! He must've spent all his leaves down here, prospectin' the Black Hills country for its hidden riches!

'Clyde knew that he could force the openin' of the Hills,' he went on, 'and when he heard from Custer that President Grant had given the order, he scotched me and hustled for the nearest land office to cinch his claims to the best spots! Even if Custer had got on his trail, for forgin' army orders, he'd been rich as Croesus and could have hid behind dummies or bought hisself out of trouble!'

'Why, that map's worth millions, General!' cried Mireles. The Kid stared at his Mexican friend, whose dark eyes gleamed.

'Huh! Fever's hit you, too, has it? Those back at Deadwood can keep what they've paid for in blood and misery. Reckon Billy North and that young girl of his'll be happy together. But Sioux gold ain't for you and me, savvy?'

He was sickened by bloodshed, by the lure that had brought forth from the slime such a murderous traitor as Hanson Clyde, with an insane lust for power and wealth.

From his pocket the Kid drew his waterproof match case, and struck a match. The little stick flared up, and the Kid deliberately held a corner of the dead Clyde's map in the flame. It took hold and the paper began smoking. It burned, blackening to nothingness. Dropping the flaming map, the

Kid added the claim papers to the fire, watching them with grim eyes.

He did not look at them again, nor at Major Clyde. Mounting the dun, and trailed by his loyal comrade Celestino Mireles, the Rio Kid swung southwest from the dark Black Hills, the hills of the Sioux that threw their mysterious summits to the sky.